CYNTHIA HICKEY

A Strange Game For Caper

A Tiny House Mystery, Book Five

By Cynthia Hickey

DEDICATION

To all my die hard readers who anxiously await the next
adventure!.

Chapter One

"Heavenly Acres has a Peeping Tom."

"What?" I glanced up from where I sat with my feet propped on my coffee table, a cup of coffee in hand, and Caper snuggled up against me on the sofa.

Mags rolled her eyes. "I do believe I spoke simple English. You know what a Peeping Tom is."

"Of course, I do. Why do you think we have one?" I scratched Caper behind her furry ear.

"I saw him looking in my window." She fell into the chair across from me. "I called Larry, but he said I'm imagining things."

"Are you?" I wiggled my eyebrows over my cup.

"Of course not. These things have to stop. There's been such a big turnover of residents in this community because of all the crime that's happened since you arrived."

Which ripped at my heart. I'd been expecting an

email stating I was being let go all winter. Instead, we'd passed through the cooler months with no felonies or misdemeanors. "Maybe things are starting to get better."

"Nope. With warmer weather people head outside. That's when the trouble starts." Mags glanced at her watch. "Are you coming to look at my flower bed for footprints or not?"

I sighed and set my cup on the table. Although I'd left the front door open to let in the spring breeze, to further show my displeasure at being interrupted by Mags, I grabbed my jacket and slammed my feet to the floor. "Come on, Caper. You might as well get some exercise." Anyone who lived around these parts knew spring could mean nice weather one day and cold the next.

Mags led the way across the street to number five. She'd recently refreshed the banana-colored paint with eggplant trim. I grimaced, wishing she'd have chosen more subtle colors. But, she owned the house, unlike most who rented, and it wasn't worth the battle.

"See?" She pointed at the freshly turned dirt of her flower bed. "I was getting ready to plant some spring flowers and spotted the footprints."

I bent over. Sure enough, the prints were clear in the fresh dirt. "I thought you said you saw someone peeking?"

"I did. That was last night. I'm not foolish enough to run out here in the dark. I waited until morning."

Not being an expert, I guessed the shoe to be a man's size ten-and-a-half or eleven. "Did you call

Davis? Now that he's married to your granddaughter, he'll tolerate our interference better than before, or you can sic Amber on him."

"You're the manager here."

"Seriously?" I frowned and pulled my cell phone from my pocket. "You should have called him before coming over. I am not law enforcement."

She laughed. "One couldn't tell with the way you get involved in dangerous police investigations."

"Not by choice." But somehow I always got dragged in. Either because a friend's name needed to be cleared or because the bad guy threatened me with knowing more than I actually did.

"What now, CJ?" Davis practically growled my name.

"Mags had someone peeking in her window last night. There are clear footprints in the dirt outside her window."

"Why are you calling me?"

"Because I'm the manager. Her words, not mine."

He sighed. "I'll send Officer Milton over." Click.

"Sending Milton." I slipped the phone back in my pocket and scanned the property for Caper.

She dug in the sand under the playground equipment, filling the air with dirt. My heart hitched for a minute since every time she became that determined, things turned bad for me. I chose not to borrow trouble, crossed the street again and climbed into my golf cart. "Want to come along on my rounds?"

Mags shook her head. "I'll wait for Milton."

"It might be a while. It isn't an emergency."

"Says you. I need to get these flowers planted."

I waved and headed around Lake Blue Waters for a quick look-through of the campgrounds. People were booking sites left and right in anticipation of crappie season. That meant Eric, my park ranger boyfriend, and I would be kept busy. Those who didn't like roughing it would be interested in the empty tiny houses I had for rent.

I spotted Eric's Gator where the trailer belonging to Robison, the former campground manager, had once stood. The burn marks still showed from where the poachers had burned the trailer to the ground months ago. I parked my golf cart next to Eric's vehicle, then strolled to the top of the hill.

Eric knelt in the dirt next to the water's edge. He waved me over when he glanced up and saw me. "Mind giving me a hand?" he asked when I stopped next to him.

"Sure. What do you need?"

"Someone warm to cuddle this little guy." He held out his hands to show me a tiny tiger-striped grey tabby. "He's cold and wet."

"What in the world?" I took the poor thing and tucked him inside my shirt.

"I found him tied to a bush. Had the darndest time getting him free. He'd jumped around until he tangled himself up real good." Eric wiped his hands on his khaki pants. "I think someone dumped him off."

"At least they left him by the water and not in it." The kitten purred against my chest. "Caper will have a new roomie."

"I thought you might want to keep him." Eric

smiled and gave me a quick one-armed hug so as not to squash the little guy. "Any idea for a name?"

"Not yet. It'll come. I'm kind of thinking of Sherlock. Maybe he'll keep Caper out of trouble."

Eric laughed. "I doubt it. Where is the little rascal?"

"Digging in the playground. I'll let her have her fun, then go fill in the holes." I nuzzled Sherlock, then spotted Milton pull up to Mags's house across the lake. "I'd better go. Mags had a peeper last night, supposedly, and had me call the cops."

"I've got some work to do around here in preparation for the busy season. I'll stop by later." He planted a kiss on my forehead and walked me back to the cart.

I sped down the path and returned to Mags's house. Milton was studying the footprints. "Look what I got?" I held up Sherlock. "Someone left him by the lake."

"Poor baby." Mags took the kitten. "I've been wanting another one."

I took him back. "Sorry, but Sherlock is mine."

"If you two would like to stop gushing over the kitten," Milton said, crossing his arms, "I have a few questions. If you saw the guy, Mags, what did he look like?"

"It was dark. I could only tell someone was there."

Noting her closed curtains, I glanced up at the streetlight. "You saw a silhouette?"

"Yes." She gave a definitive nod.

"Keep your doors and windows locked and let us know if the person comes back." Milton snapped a picture of the footprints, patted Sherlock, then headed back to his squad car. Before opening the door, he glanced back. "What is in your dog's mouth?"

I turned to see Caper, long ears flapping, run toward us. She stopped and dropped a bag of white powder at my feet, then barked.

We all froze, then I reached down to pick it up.

"Don't touch that." Milton put a hand on my arm. He snapped a glove on his hand, then lifted the bag and opened it. "Where did she get this?"

"What is it?" I asked.

"I think it's cocaine."

"Why is my dog always bringing me gifts of drugs or priceless gems?" My heart skipped a beat, threatening to stop altogether. Every time Caper brought me a gift, I ended up running from a killer.

Chapter Two

"Where did it come from?" Milton asked again.

"Caper's been digging in the playground." I glanced wide-eyed in that direction as Sage Flower pulled another bag from a hole.

He held it out to his sister, Rose. "Sugar."

"No!" Milton bellowed, running as fast as his rather overweight body would allow. "Put that down."

Mags and I peered at each other and darted after him. Sherlock meowed from under my shirt. Poor thing. Welcome to my world.

Milton snatched the bag from Sage's six-year-old hands and ordered his sister to take him home. He glared at me as if this was all my fault, then returned to his squad car to retrieve crime-scene tape.

"You're closing off the playground?" Where would the children play?

"Until we know there's no more drugs, yes."

"Maybe it is sugar and flour," Mags said. "You haven't tested it yet."

"Even you aren't that naïve." He handed me the end of the tape. "Hold this. It isn't some kind of game, ladies. This is dangerous."

By the time the tape encircled the playground, a crowd of looky-loos had gathered. Roy Olson, the area's all-around handyman, stopped his cart next to me. "What happened? Another murder?"

"No, thank God. Just drugs."

"Who dug all those holes I'm going to have to fill back up?"

"Caper."

"Ah." He nodded, not surprised at the trouble my dog caused on a regular basis.

Within the hour, a truck pulled up with men wearing gloves and armed with shovels. If I thought Caper dug a lot of holes, I'd been mistaken. Pretty soon, the playground looked like a prairie dog village and multiple bags of drugs lay in a pile.

"How did all this get here with no one noticing?" I frowned.

"That's the mystery now, isn't it?" Mags patted my shoulder. "Things aren't looking good for you as manager. I'd be expecting a pink slip any day."

"Do you ever filter the words that come out of your mouth?" I glared.

She shrugged. "I guess not."

Lucy Flower marched in my direction, her brood of kids trailing behind her. I still hadn't figured out how a family of six lived comfortably in a tiny house. The woman must have superb organization skills. "My son could have died." She crossed her arms.

"I'm sorry, but I didn't put the drugs there." I could see the little we'd worked together to shut down a deer-poaching ring didn't mean a whole lot to her. I was seriously doubting my managerial position. It didn't help with all the bad things that had happened as mentioned by Mags. I needed more coffee and a trip to the pet store.

Davis pulled up and shook his head at me before climbing out of his car. I sighed and headed home. I'd had enough.

Instead of going home, I veered off and took the trail to the chapel in the woods, my pride and joy since having it restored. I pushed open the door we never locked, not wanting anyone to feel excluded from the peace inside. I sat in the front row, Caper next to me, sniffing my shirt. I smiled and set Sherlock on the polished seat of the pew.

"Be nice, Caper." She didn't care for Mags's cat, Callie, but I hoped she'd do better with this one.

I sat back, stretched my arms along the back of the pew, and promised myself I wouldn't get involved in another mystery. Surely my luck at outrunning killers was running out. My gaze fell on the simple cross in front of me. Who was I kidding? With my reputation as manager of Heavenly Acres at stake, I had to find out who planted the drugs and how they managed to get away with it with no one seeing them.

The door opened behind me. I smiled, recognizing Eric's footsteps. He sat beside me. "I thought I'd find you here when you weren't home."

"More than one person has accused me of negligence." I rested my head on his shoulder.

"Don't listen. You are definitely not negligent. Look at all you've done since being hired. Security cameras, landscaping—the place is definitely better than before."

"Escalating crime, deaths…" I had a list of my own.

"If your mysterious boss didn't think you capable, you wouldn't be handling registrations for the campground in addition to Heavenly Acres. I, for one, appreciate your help." He kissed the top of my head. "You're going to get involved, aren't you?"

I straightened and faced him. "How can I not? Someone buried a lot of drugs right under my nose—no pun intended."

"What do you want to do first?" He closed his eyes, resigned.

"I need to talk to every person who rented a house within the last few months. It has to have happened during the winter months when the playground wasn't used as much." I always thought better in the chapel. With no distractions, my mind could actually formulate a plan. "It won't be hard to make a list once I'm on my laptop."

"I can help by going through the camp registrations. There weren't many during the cold weather." He gave me a sideways hug. "But I don't want any more treks through the woods or high-speed chases. My poor jeep has just recovered from the last time."

Not to mention the arm that was broken when the poachers ran him off the road. "I'll do my best not to do those things." I smiled and scooped up the kitten as it tried to jump off the pew. "Want to come with me to the pet store?"

"I can't. There's some poison ivy growing in one of the sites I need to take care of." He gave me a quick kiss. "I'll bring over Chinese for supper."

"Sounds yummy." Still holding Sherlock, I called Caper to come and followed Eric outside. He gave me a ride to my car and another kiss.

I glanced to where men still worked at the playground, then set Sherlock on the front passenger seat with Caper and started the car. Sherlock immediately yowled and leaped on my head.

My screams would have awakened the dead because Milton came running, gun drawn, and yanked open the driver side door. "What is it?"

"Get it off!" I grappled for Sherlock whose claws clutched my hair.

Milton laughed and plucked the kitten from my head. "Cats don't like car rides. You need a carrier."

"I see that." I rubbed my head and tried patting my hair back into some semblance of order. "Will you see if Mags has one?" I reached my hands out to take back my devil kitten.

"Sure." Still laughing, he jogged to Mags's house and returned a few minutes later with a cat carrier.

I sported more scratches trying to get Sherlock into the carrier. Cats were definitely not as docile as dogs. By the time we arrived at the pet store, my head pounded from the kitten's howling, and I vowed car trips with a feline would be rare. I set the carrier into the shopping basket along with Caper and tried to ignore all the stares because of the siren-like sounds coming from my cat. I bought more items than I probably needed, not taking the time to think about what I should or shouldn't buy and almost ran to the register.

"That is one unhappy kitten," the girl at the register said.

"He's had a rough day." I quickly paid and sped home where I was more than happy to let Sherlock loose. I set up his litter box in the tiny bathroom and showed him where it was, then fixed myself my third cup of coffee of the day and wished I was a wine drinker. Instead, I sat on the sofa and propped my feet on the coffee table in almost the exact posture I'd been in when this horrible day had started. Caper curled up on one side of me, Sherlock the other. I smiled and watched through the window as the men working on the playground climbed into their truck and left.

Yellow crime-scene tape fluttered in the wind. The flower children and Danny Olson stood outside of it. How long before one of them broke the law and ducked under the tape?

Danny and Rose talked, laughed, then high-fived each other. I knew the teenagers well enough to know they'd just come up with an idea that would not be approved by either of their parents. I sighed, knowing I'd have to see what they were up to.

"Life was easier when Grams was alive." I played with Caper's ears thinking back. For years I'd been my grandmother's caretaker. When she'd died, not having the heart to stay in her house, I'd taken this job. My friend and former police officer, Ann Lowery, now rented the house and took good care of it for me.

Seeing I had an hour before Eric would arrive

with supper, I finished my coffee and went in search of the wayward teens. I found them at the picnic table in front of the Olson house, heads together whispering.

I snuck up behind them. "Hey."

Rose shrieked.

Danny jumped to his feet, fists doubled. "I could have punched you."

"I would have hit you back." I grinned and sat across from them. "What are you two up to, and don't dare lie to me."

"What makes you think we're planning something?" Danny sat back down.

"Yeah." Rose narrowed her eyes.

"You're always up to something, and drugs buried in the sand is bound to have gotten your curiosity up." I folded my hands on the tabletop and arched a brow. "Well?"

"Remember when my dad entered the deer hunt competition?" Danny crossed his arms. "He hired some landscapers to help out around here."

"I didn't know that."

He shrugged. "You were busy trying to find out who killed Mr. Robinson. Anyway, Rose and I think they have to be the ones who buried the drugs because they were the only non-regulars who had access and wouldn't have been questioned."

I pressed my lips together and thought for a minute. "That was months ago. Why hasn't anyone retrieved the bags? They have to be worth a lot of money."

"Maybe something happened to the men," Rose said softly. "Like someone killed them in a drug fight."

"Yeah." Danny nodded. "Now no one knows where they're buried. But word will get out about the bust. A news helicopter buzzed around here when you were in town."

Which meant someone would come looking for whatever might still be there, undiscovered. I glanced toward the playground. Whatever was still there, I needed to get it away from Heavenly Acres.

Chapter Three

"What am I doing?" I glanced at Caper on the golf cart seat next to me the next morning. "Am I seriously contemplating breaking the law—again—by disregarding the crime-scene tape and letting you loose?" Because I knew if I put her down, she'd run right under the tape and start digging. Considering all the holes in the playground, chances of her finding anything were slim, but if something was there undiscovered, her little black nose would sniff it out.

"You're taking our suggestion seriously, aren't you?" Danny stopped on his way to the bus stop, backpack slung over one shoulder.

I nodded. "Did you get the names of the grounds crew?"

He pulled a sheet of paper from his pocket. "Rose did. Said her uncle needed someone, so Dad gave her the names easy enough."

"You'll make a good detective someday." I smiled, taking the paper. I'd research the names on my laptop when I returned home.

The boy grinned and trotted to catch the bus that had just pulled up to the gate. I stared at the flapping tape for a few more seconds, then started my daily drive around the community. The sight of so many empty houses cast a pall of depression over me. How could I find tenants, good ones, who didn't know or care about our recent rash of murders and robberies? I still hadn't emailed my boss about the torn-up playground or the reason for the destruction.

I stopped the cart in front of the new number ten. A white house with navy-blue trim. I hadn't wanted to replace the house, since it seemed cursed always to have residents up to no good, but my phantom boss had insisted. He—or she—had told me not to be superstitious. He said that houses were inanimate objects and incapable of wrongdoing. I wasn't quite as sure.

By the time I circled around, Mags was working in her flower bed. "Good morning."

She straightened and peered up from under her floppy hat. "Good morning. What are you up to today?"

I told her about my conversation the day before with Danny and Rose. "Want to place a bet the names don't exist?"

"Nope." She waved a hand shovel at me. "Just like that phony house rental place a few months back. It will be nothing more than a fake front for nefarious means. Where's the kitten?"

"After the car ride yesterday, I didn't think he'd like the golf cart any better."

"If you're going to let your troublesome dog ride with you, then you should train the kitten to do the same. It ain't fair."

I chuckled and drove home to give my mistreated kitty a treat. Which meant I had to give one to Caper. I started to feel as if I had two children rather than pets. Fur babies taken care of, I settled myself on the sofa and opened my laptop. First I emailed my boss and prayed I wouldn't be fired, then started researching the names. Sure enough, they didn't exist. I tried switching first names with last names. Still nothing. How could I find out more? I called Ann. "You busy?"

"I'm on surveillance and bored out of my mind. I hate watching cheating spouses cheat. What's up?"

"Did you hear about the drugs buried at Heavenly Acres?"

"Sure did. People are wondering how that happened without anyone seeing."

"I'm wondering the same." I explained about the grounds crew. "Any recent deaths of three men who might have been kept hushed or downplayed?"

"Let me call my contact and get back to you." Click.

Was I the only person left in the world that said "bye" before hanging up? While I waited for Ann to call me back, I tossed a ball for Caper and rolled one with a bell in it for Sherlock. With a house of only a few hundred square feet, the balls were returned quickly. My phone rang just as boredom started to set in.

"Tell me you got something," I said.

"I did." I could hear Ann's grin across the airwaves. "Supposedly, the deaths of three John Does were pushed to the back burner during the poaching spree. By the time the poachers were caught, no one came forth about missing persons or responded to the men's descriptions that were given on the news once or twice. If their prints were in the system, my contact doesn't know."

"Do you think they're the men I'm looking for?"

"I'd bet my house."

"My house, you mean, and please don't bet it. How did the men die?"

"Execution-style shooting."

So, Danny's and Rose's imaginations were closer to the truth than any of us had thought. "I don't want to get involved this time."

She laughed. "You say that every time, and yet I end up having to save your rear end."

"Sometimes I save myself." I rolled my eyes so far back in my head I got a glimpse of my brain. I had the information I'd sought but didn't have a clue as to what to do with it. "It's still speculation but also clear that those men probably buried drugs on the playground while doing work around here. What I don't know is who killed them or why?"

"I'll let Davis know what we found out and leave it to him to deal with. Oh, the man I'm watching is leaving. Gotta go." Click.

I settled back on the sofa, proud of a productive day and not even noon yet. I'd turned into a pretty good investigator during my time at Heavenly Acres.

"You're looking pleased with yourself." Davis frowned from my open doorway. "What have I told you about leaving your door open?"

"I'm training Sherlock not to go outside." I shrugged. "Besides, no one wants to kill me."

"Yet." He sighed and sat across from me. "Ann told me what you've discovered. Rather than you run off half-cocked, I thought I should fill you in on some of the details. Not all. Just a few so you know why you need to stay out of this one."

"Okay." I clutched Sherlock to my chest, not sure I wanted to hear any details. Once he told me, it would be harder not to get involved.

"Three men, two Hispanic, one Caucasian, were found shot behind the grocery store four months ago. Right after the poaching."

"Related?"

"I doubt it. Poachers and drug dealers are different sorts of people."

Not necessarily true. I'd run into both, and both wanted to kill anyone who got in their way.

"The three men all have criminal records. We knew their identities before asking someone to come forth and claim their bodies. No one did, so we went with the John Doe theory in hopes of drawing the crooks out of hiding."

"Didn't work?"

"Not yet. Once we announce the discovery of the bags of cocaine, the perps will come out." He sat back, his forehead creased. "With your reputation of putting your nose where it doesn't belong, I'm afraid they'll want to put you out of commission before you can butt in."

My blood ran cold. "You're saying that even if I don't get involved, I'm in danger? Why? You have to have a reason."

"The footprint found outside of Mags's house matched the tread found at the scene of the shooting.

You have the same footprints outside of your house. Milton checked."

"That puts Mags in danger, too."

He nodded. "I'm asking the two of you to move into your grandmother's house with Ann. Just until we catch these guys. You can't stay here. These houses are too small."

Especially since we'd have a dog and two cats. My shoulders slumped. "Have you told Mags yet?"

His mouth quirked. "I'm hoping you'll go with me as protection."

"Smart man." I stood and glanced around my house. "I'll still have to work, you know. I'll spend the nights with Ann, but I'll be back here each day."

"During daylight hours only and never alone. Either Ann or your uncle will accompany you."

I sighed. If I had to keep hiring Ann, I'd go bankrupt. "Let's go break the bad news."

"Absolutely not," Mags said, crossing her arms when we told her. "Short of physically removing me, you can't make me leave."

Larry stepped out of her house. "I'll carry you out."

"Let me stay with you."

He shook his head. "I've decided to stay with you women." He grinned. "We'll be cozy, packed into that three-bedroom house."

My gaze landed on the pistol on his hip. Life used to be so peaceful. "I'll go pack what I need and meet you there."

"I'll stay until you're packed," Davis said. "Larry can watch over Mags."

"Does Eric know?" I asked on the way to my

house.

"Yes. He's on the mountain but will see you later."

Leaving Davis downstairs, I climbed the loft and pulled a suitcase from under my bed. I tossed in clothes, my pepper spray, my laptop, and any files I might need in order to do my job from town. Since I'd be back each day, it wasn't a big deal if I forgot something. I put an unhappy Sherlock into his carrier, clipped the leash on Caper, and put their pet food and supplies into a box. With one last glance around my house, hoping I'd see it again, I locked the front door on my way out.

As I put my pets and things into my Prius, Davis informed me he'd follow me to Ann's. The seriousness of the situation, the fact he'd taken time out of his day to warn me and escort me, told me how much danger he believed I was in. All this, and I hadn't even started to investigate in earnest as I'd done in the past.

I would now. The sooner those people were behind bars, the sooner I could resume my life.

Chapter Four

With a howling cat, a sleeping dog, and a police detective following me, I drove to my grandmother's/Ann's house. Ann waited on the front porch.

"I cleaned out the master bedroom for you," she said.

"No need. It's your house as long as you're paying rent. I'm only a guest." I inhaled deeply through my nose and entered the house where I'd cared for Grams for so long. Rather than take the room Ann offered, I headed for the room I'd slept in while here. The last room would be for Mags and her devil cat.

I set Sherlock's carrier on the bed and let him out. He immediately darted off the bed and under it. No problem. I put his litter box in the corner, set out his toys, and let Caper follow me outside to get the rest of our things.

"That determined set of your shoulders tells me you aren't going to take this sitting down." Ann shook her head. "You're going to bring danger to our doorstep again."

I whirled. "I didn't start this. If my life has to be disrupted, then someone is going to pay." Hopefully, it wouldn't be me or someone I cared about. I grabbed my suitcase from the car and stalked back into the house.

"CJ—" Davis warned. "Stay. Out. Of. It. Let me handle things."

"Sure." I dropped the suitcase on the faded blue bedspread.

Not much had changed in my room, color-wise anyway. The off-white dresser and desk sat empty. No clothes hung in the small closet. No posters of teen heartthrobs hung on the walls. Yet, the feeling of having reverted back to young adulthood almost overwhelmed me. Was this feeling why I hadn't chosen to live there? If so, why couldn't I bring myself to sell the house? I ran my hand over the comforter. Because I loved this place. It had been a place of safety and love. Being made to return under these circumstances threatened all that.

"Are you okay?"

I glanced up and smiled at Eric. "I thought you were away."

"I was." He entered and sat next to me. "I felt you needed me more than my job does right now." Putting his arm around me, he pulled me close.

"When I lived here, I sat on this bed and wished my life was more exciting. I had no idea how exciting it would get."

He laughed. "Be careful what you wish for."

"For sure. Danger keeps at me like a dog trying

to get the last morsel of food from under the sofa."

"Come on." He stood and held out his hand. "I brought pizza for lunch."

Until he mentioned food, I hadn't realized how hungry I was. Even Sherlock ventured out from under the bed and streaked toward the dining room. "Let's eat and make plans."

He groaned and pulled me after him. "You're going to give me gray hair."

"You'll look distinguished."

"Ha."

The others, minus Davis, who said he had work to do according to Mags, already held slices of pepperoni pizza in their hands.

Larry held out the box. "I hope you ladies don't mind, but I'll be sleeping on the sofa while we're here."

"That makes me feel better about the situation." Eric grabbed a slice and sat down. "I'd stay too, but I need to remain close to watch the campground."

"Which I should be doing." I chose a slice.

"You're second in command," he reminded me. "You're only to be there when I can't. I'll make sure to schedule at least half of my day there."

"I'll be working at Heavenly Acres every day." I glanced around the group, daring anyone to argue with me. "If Ann or Larry wants to tag along fine, but you'll do it because you want to, not because you're being paid." I eyed Ann.

"Then I'll have to accept other work." She narrowed her eyes. "I have bills to pay. Maybe you should come along with me sometime."

"Maybe I will." I gave a cheeky grin. "With as

much trouble as I'm always in, paying you to be my bodyguard will put me in the poorhouse."

"Why are you being so obstinate?" Mags picked up Callie from the floor. "Ann needs money."

Ann's eyebrows almost disappeared into her hairline. "I'm doing fine, thank you."

"You just said—" Mags rolled her eyes. "I'm trying to take up for you."

"CJ and I are only joking around. I'm more than happy to help watch over her as a friend."

"I'm right here." I glanced from Mags to Ann. "No need to talk about me as if I'm not.

Sherlock jumped on the table. I scooped him up and put him on the floor. He jumped right back up, grabbed a piece of pepperoni off my plate and dashed away with a barking Caper on his heels. Hershey, Eric's dog, who was lying under the table, gave chase, knocking a lamp off a side table.

"This is a mad house." Mags kissed the top of Callie's head. "My poor baby will be anxious. I'll have to give her meds."

I had a feeling I'd be the one needing meds before all was said and done.

"I'm a little envious," Eric said. "Y'all together will be like one big party all day and night. Popcorn and movies, pet antics. Yep, it sounds like a good time."

"Don't forget the wine," Mags said. "We're going to need it."

Joking aside, I brought up the real reason we resembled a fraternity house. "How do we draw these people we know nothing about into the open so the police can catch them?"

It was like I'd dumped ice water on their heads. The laughter and jokes stopped immediately.

Larry scratched his chin. "Without spreading the word you have something the cops missed, I can't think of anything."

I did plan on letting Caper do some more digging. Kind of like a strange game of finding the hidden treasure. From the destruction of the playground, though, I doubted anything had been left behind. "We need to find out more about the fake gardeners. Why were they executed? Did they betray someone or did someone betray them?"

"Tough questions," Ann said. "I'll see what I can find out from my source."

"We need to meet this source of yours." I wiggled my eyebrows. "I think you like him."

"Who said it was a him?"

"Isn't it?"

Her cheeks darkened. "Yes, but if I introduce him to all of you, then Davis will know where I get my inside information."

"He works at the precinct?" My hand with the pizza halted halfway to my mouth.

"It isn't Milton, is it?" Mags's eyes widened.

"Heavens no." Ann shook her head. "He isn't a cop."

"The plot thickens. He's the IT guy." I bit my bottom lip, knowing I was right despite the vigorous shake of her head.

"Can we get back to the task at hand, please?" Ann stood and started cleaning up the empty plates and pizza boxes.

"Sure." I was happy for her. It was time my friend

found someone. Too bad she felt compelled to keep him secret.

"Does this house have security?" Larry asked.

"No, I've never needed it."

"I'll install motion-sensor cameras tomorrow and alarms on the doors and windows. Whoever might be threatening you and Mags could take you both out at once since you're living under the same roof. Davis didn't think this through." He drummed his fingers on the table.

"Maybe he wanted us together to make it easier on him," I suggested. "Unless someone knows my background, they won't know I own this house."

"That won't be hard to find out." Eric scratched behind Hershey's ears. "I wonder who managed to get the piece of pepperoni."

"My bet is on Caper." I grinned. "She's the real troublemaker here."

"I'd best get back to work." Eric stood. "I'll be doing a lot of back and forth in the upcoming weeks."

"I'll walk you out."

"Just to the door."

Good grief. Did he think the bad guys were waiting out front for me to step outside?

At the door, he turned and kissed me. "Text me every half hour as to where you are."

"I'll try to remember. Can't you look at the tracker on my phone?"

"Yes, but I want to hear from you." He flashed a grin, called to his dog, and jogged to his jeep.

I sighed and closed the door, wondering for at least the hundredth time how a man like him could love a woman like me. A woman who kept the world around her in constant turmoil. Eric went around helping people and keeping the world around him beautiful. While I wanted the same thing, we definitely went about it differently.

Rather than join the others as they moved to the living room, I let Caper out into the backyard to do her business. I couldn't guarantee she wouldn't make her own holes, but I patrolled the perimeter of the quarter-of-an-acre lot making sure there weren't any holes under the fence she could escape through.

This had been Caper's home for the first year of her life before I'd inherited the dog and moved her to a house the size of the master bedroom. Caper didn't seem to mind. She was happy wherever I was.

I leaned on the chain-link fence at the back of the yard and stared into the trees. A large long-horn bull came into view seeming as startled to see me as I was him. After watching me with his dark eyes for a few seconds, he lowered his massive head and grazed. It moved silently for one so big.

Which meant... I stiffened. If a bull could sneak up on me, then so could a person. A chain-link fence was no protection at all. Movement to my right caught my eye. A black snake slithered toward me.

I screamed and raced for the house.

Eric and Larry bolted out the door. "What happened?" they asked in unison.

"A snake." I pointed and hid behind Eric.

"A rat snake." Larry frowned. "Totally harmless."

A snake was a snake. I'd rather face a psycho with a gun than a snake.

Chapter Five

By morning, I'd decided to take my chances. A privacy fence would spoil the view. Larry had already scheduled men to come and install cameras which he could monitor from his laptop. He would be able to warn me if trouble came stalking through the woods.

I closed the bedroom door to keep Sherlock contained and carried Caper to where Ann waited by the front door. Today, I wanted my nosy pup to search the area around the playground rather than the other side of the crime-scene tape. The grounds crew had been all over Heavenly Acres. If I wanted to hide something as they had, I'd make sure to spread it out.

I also woke worried about my job. I never received a response to the email about the drugs buried around Heavenly Acres. Sighing, I mentioned it to Ann as we drove to work.

"Why don't you just ask him?" She cut me a sideways look.

"I did. He didn't respond to my email. Wait." I

almost got whiplash turning from the window to her. "How do you know the owner is a he?"

"Are you serious?" She blinked like an owl. "A girl as smart as you, one who catches killers on a regular basis, and you haven't figured it out?"

"Stop playing games."

"Heavenly *Acres*. Who do you know with that name?" She rolled her eyes. "Gee whiz, girl."

"Oh, my gosh. Larry Acres." My uncle was the owner. He'd known about me far longer than I even knew he existed.

"Ding ding ding! You win a prize." She turned her car onto the Interstate, her gaze going to the rearview mirror.

I glanced behind us. "Are we being followed?"

"Not yet, but we snuck out without Mags. I guarantee you she'll have Larry bring her so she doesn't miss anything."

"We should have brought her with us."

Ann shook her head. "We're safer split up. That way, anyone targeting us can't take us all out at once."

A shiver ran through me, and I hugged Caper a little harder. "You're expecting this to get bad."

"Unfortunately, yes."

"What if we took a vacation?"

"The problem would still be here when we returned."

I exhaled hard enough to ruffle Caper's fur. Ann was right. What really burned my bacon was that I'd done absolutely nothing to put a target on my back and still couldn't believe what had been done right under my nose. If my newly-discovered uncle didn't own the place, I'd be fired.

I breathed a sigh of relief when we pulled into the community. My tiny house still sat where I'd left it. Eric's jeep sat outside of his house, but the Gator was gone. A far-off roar of its engine told me he was patrolling the campground. Good, because he'd try to talk me out of setting Caper loose.

"Spill it. I know you've got something going on inside your head." Ann shoved her car door open.

"I'm taking Caper for a walk." I grinned and headed to where the playground ended. Where else? The common area.

The community was comprised of a large circle surrounding a common area and playground, separated by flowering bushes. With the playground torn up, the common area was the next best place to dig before heading to the water's edge.

I set Caper down. "Find the stuff, girl."

"What do you plan on doing with the stuff if she does find more?" Ann raised her eyebrows. "Withholding information from the police is a crime."

"I know. My plan is to draw the drug dealers into the open, make a deal with them, and have the authorities swoop in and save the day." It sounded like a good plan, even when spoken out loud. "Someone will see Caper digging and know exactly why. I don't doubt for a second that we aren't being watched right now."

"By whom? You know all the tenants." Ann glanced around.

Larry's truck pulled next to us. Mags glared at us through the window before opening her door and climbing out. "You two are the meanest people I know. Tell them how angry I am, Larry."

"You just did, sweetheart." His gaze flicked to Caper. "I don't like this."

I crossed my arms and hiked my chin. "You're the boss. You can always order me to quit."

Rather than look guilty, he seemed rather pleased. "I thought you'd figure it out sooner than later."

"Why didn't you tell me?"

"Tell you what?" Mags glanced from me to him.

"That my dear uncle is the eccentric that owns Heavenly Acres." I tilted my head. "Why the secrecy?"

"I was afraid you wouldn't take the job and after my…mother died, well, I wanted you taken care of."

My uncle, my mother's half-brother, had been raised by his paternal grandparents after his father, Grams's first love, died in the war. He'd looked me up and offered me a job.

Tears pricked my eyes. "I'm not qualified for this. I've done nothing but bring trouble here."

He put his hands on my shoulders and peered into my eyes. "That is a lie, Clarice Josephine. It was your kindness in caring for my mother that led me to hire you when you applied for the job. That simple application led me to the discovery of a wonderful niece." He smiled. "You do have a penchant for getting into trouble, but what has befallen this place is not your fault. It's simply a case of extremely bad luck."

"Really?"

He pulled me in for a hug. "Really."

Mags sniffed and wiped away a tear. "I wish I had recorded this tender moment."

"I'm more curious about what Caper is doing," Ann said.

I stepped back from Larry and searched for my dog. She wasn't digging. Instead, she ran in circles making small yipping sounds. "Something's wrong." I darted toward her. It took some effort, but eventually I caught her.

A swarm of red ants streaked up my arms and started biting. "She got into ants." I raced for the lake and jumped in.

Icy water closed over my head. Caper struggled to get free, adding scratches to the bites on my arms. It wasn't until I sloshed through the water and mud that I realized I'd jumped in with my phone in my pocket.

Caper shook the water from her fur, then glanced up at me. "What?" I frowned. "You didn't get a bath." I always gave her a doggie treat after a bathing. "Oh, come on. I need to change anyway."

"Put that phone in rice immediately," Mags said. "Blow dry, then rice."

I waved at her, entered my house, and went straight to my loft. Using a blow dryer, I blew the phone dry, grabbed some clothes, and stomped down to the kitchen where I put rice and the phone into a Ziplock baggie, then changed into dry clothes. When I'd finished, I tossed Caper a treat.

"Why weren't you digging?" I put my hands on my hips. "If I didn't want you to, you'd have dug up every inch of ground in sight. But, no, you have to get into an ant pile."

"Could be worse," Ann said entering the house. "She could have tangled with a skunk."

True. I plopped onto the sofa and tried to remember if anything was on the day's agenda. Nope. Nada. Not a thing. Ugh. Heavenly Acres was going to fail, and despite Larry's assurances to the contrary, I felt responsible.

"What are you doing?" Ann stood over me.

"Feeling sorry for myself. My arms burn."

"Put some medicine on them and get back to work. You'll never be back in your own home acting this way, and I like living by myself." She glanced at her phone screen. "I need to take this." She stepped outside.

I didn't mean to eavesdrop, but she was definitely talking to her contact. A few minutes later, she returned. "I've got the last known address of our grounds crew. Turns out they really did landscape work. The drug thing was a side job."

"Where do they live?" I sat up.

"The trailer park at the edge of town."

Asking questions around there would stir things up. "Let's go."

The screaming of children drew me outside. The Flower boys raced down the road while holding tight to a kite string. Why weren't they in school?

"Briar, Sage, come here." I motioned with my pointer finger.

The two boys stared up at me with wide eyes and jelly smears on their faces. "Ma'am," Briar, the ten-year-old and older of the two said.

"Why aren't the two of you in school?"

"We're sick," Sage said, puffing out his chest.

"You don't look sick." Ann folded her arms. "Truancy is against the law, you know."

The boys glanced at each other, then Briar back at us. "I guess since I don't know what that word means, we ain't doing it."

"It means skipping school." I shook my head but couldn't hide my grin. They were adorable and the warm sunshine and gentle breeze were perfect for kite flying. "Where's your mother?"

"Taking a nap. We'd better be home before she wakes up."

I doubted whether she'd be fooled but nodded. "It's getting close to nine o'clock. She'll be getting up soon."

They dashed home, the kite banging on the ground behind them.

"I don't like that they're unsupervised," Ann said.

"Lucy works long hours. The boys look out for each other. They're healthy, fed, with a roof over their heads." I'd been concerned once too, but after getting to know the family, my concerns eased.

Caper lay under the outdoor picnic table, clearly not interested in the whole reason I'd brought her. I shook my head and climbed into the golf cart. "Come on, girl." When she opened one eye and didn't move, I had Ann clip her leash on her so she couldn't wander off. "See you later."

Ann climbed into the cart and we made a slow circle around the grounds. Other than the torn-up playground, everything looked in order. Wait a minute. I stopped in front of number twenty. A fresh pot of flowers sat in front of the house.

"There's no reservation for this place."

"Maybe Roy took it," Ann said.

"It's not part of his job." I turned off the cart and slid out.

"I'll go first." Ann stepped in front of me, hand on the gun at her hip.

"It's a tenant, not a drug lord."

"You don't know that."

I moved past her and up the stairs, fist raised to knock. The door opened before I could. I stared into the smiling face of an elderly woman.

"Hello? How may I help you?"

"I'm the manager here, and I don't recall renting this house to you. May I ask when you arrived?"

"Last night. I don't need a contract, dear. My grandson owns this place."

"You're my uncle's grandmother?"

She nodded. "He said I could pick any house I wanted. The one I shared with my husband is far too big. Would you like a cookie?"

"No, thank you. It's nice to meet you, Mrs. Acres." Larry needed to stop with the secrets. "I hope you enjoy your stay."

"I'm sure I will." She closed the door.

"Has anyone told you that life around you is never boring?" Ann asked.

"Eric says that all the time." As I headed back to the golf cart, Briar and Sage ran toward us.

"I found more sugar." Sage held up a bag of white powder.

Chapter Six

I immediately contacted the newspaper, then a few minutes later Davis. I thought it best if the news reporter showed up first.

I wanted whoever was looking for the drugs to come get them. Hopefully, they'd start digging. This time, I'd be watching. Foolish? Definitely, but enough was enough. This was my home, my people, and I wouldn't let them be endangered this way. "When this is all over, I wanted a coded gate around this community."

Ann stared at me as if I'd sprouted a third arm. "Roy would have let the grounds crew in anyway."

"I know that." I scowled. "But I guarantee you these bags weren't planted in broad daylight."

"You have a death wish." Larry shook his head and surveyed the five bags piled beside the road.

Ten minutes later, a news van sped through the gate and stopped a few feet from us. An over-eager female reporter rushed toward me and shoved a microphone in my face. "You located more bags?

Tell me about that."

I mentioned the first haul from the playground, then told her I wasn't exactly sure where these last five came from, but that they were found by some of the residents. "I'm sure there are more buried around here somewhere." I smiled at the camera. "It's like a treasure hunt. Somebody likes to play strange games, right?"

One look at Davis's face when he arrived sent the reporter and crew back to their van with the promise I'd be on the nightly news.

"Are you trying to get killed?" Davis glared. "I told you the type of people you're dealing with."

"What if we hadn't caught Sage before he tried tasting what he thought was sugar? Somebody out there knows where every bag is hidden or has a good idea. I want them to come and try taking them back before a child dies." I crossed my arms, matching his stance. "Yes, I'm putting myself in the scope of danger, but I don't see any other way."

"There's only one way and that's for you to leave this to the authorities." He paced in front of me. "Your luck is bound to run out sometime, CJ."

I nodded, fully aware that might happen. "Better me than one of my friends. It's my lack of diligence that allowed this to happen."

He froze and narrowed his eyes. "You think this is your fault?"

"I should have paid better attention. My heart almost stopped when Sage held up that bag." I'd never have forgiven myself if he'd eaten some.

"You were busy trying not to be killed by poachers." He waved his arms around. "Where's

Eric? Maybe he can talk some sense into you."

My hero rode up on his Gator, took one look at me and patted the seat next to him. "Come here. I think my girl needs a minute."

"I do indeed. The chapel, please." I sat next to him and off we went. Davis's voice trailed after us that he hadn't given me permission to leave and why didn't anyone listen to him and he should start arresting us for driving him crazy.

I almost felt sorry for him. I also knew that if he wasn't married to Mags's granddaughter, I'd have been arrested multiple times for interfering and obstruction. "How did you know I needed you?" I glanced at Eric.

"I always know." He winked. "I saw the news van, then Davis pulled up, and the van sped away. Who else would be at the center of all that excitement?" He cut the engine at the start of the path leading to the chapel.

Holding hands we strolled along the edge of the lake. The sun kissed the water's surface. A boat with a lone man fishing floated in the center. A family of mallards swam next to the long grasses. Peaceful, beautiful, and in danger of being permanently tarnished by a wave of crime rarely seen in our small town.

"Do you think it's all connected somehow?" I asked. "All the things that have gone wrong since my arrival? Thefts, poaching, diamond thieves, drug lords—? Could there be a single person or group responsible for it all?"

"Like a gang?" Eric cut me a sharp glance.

I nodded. "It would explain why trouble doesn't

go away. We haven't caught those at the top. Someone wants to claim this area to do their evil deeds." I felt in my gut I was onto something.

He opened the door to the chapel. "It's possible, I guess. There's been some activity further up the mountain that seems suspicious. No marijuana or poppy fields like we found next to the river, but a lot more four-wheeler tracks than I've ever seen."

"If we find out who's at the top of this crime spree, we can end it." I sat in the front pew. "I used to grumble about the lack of excitement in my life. Now I have too much. I'd like a happy medium."

He chuckled and sat next to me, taking my hand again. "I'm not sure that's possible with you."

"You didn't know me before." I smiled, then rested my head on his shoulder and let the peace of the place take away the stress of the morning. Afterward, I'd apologize to Davis and tell him my theory.

If I was right, the leaders couldn't be far away. Not the way everything seemed to center around Heavenly Acres and the campground. Robinson, the former caretaker of the campground, had been onto something with the poachers. His clues had enabled us to find out their identities. I couldn't help but wonder whether he'd known even more.

"You're supposed to be relaxing," Eric whispered. "Let the stress go."

I exhaled long and slow, closing my eyes and trying to let my mind go blank. It didn't work. My brain was fixated on my latest theory. "Since this isn't going to work today, we might as well return to our jobs." I stood. "What did I pull you away from?"

"I was getting ready to follow a set of new tracks. I'd ask you to come along, but being in the woods would put you in danger. Too many hiding places for the bad guys."

"I want to think on my new idea anyway. Run it past Davis and Ann. I also need to have a serious talk with Larry." I explained about him being the owner and moving in his grandmother, all without telling me.

"It does seem odd that he would keep those a secret." Eric's brow furrowed. "What's the harm in telling you?"

"Beats me."

Eric drove me home and left me with a kiss hot enough to melt concrete. "See you tonight." He tossed me a wink and drove away.

"Feel better?" Ann smirked.

"I do, thank you." I looked around, noticing the bags were gone. "Davis left?"

"Yep."

"Up to paying him a visit? I have a theory I'd like to run past the two of you."

"Okay."

I unhooked Caper from her line and carried her to Ann's car. Minutes later, we headed back to town and to the police station only to be informed that Davis wouldn't return for about an hour.

"You might as well tell me over a burger," Ann said. "Then I can tell you whether you're wasting the detective's time."

"Sneaky way of finding out first, but all right. We need a place where we can sit outside so I don't leave Caper in the car. She hates that and barks the whole time." Which is what she was doing when we stepped back outside.

"What do you do with her when it's too hot?" Ann grimaced at the shrill yapping.

"Leave her home." Sometimes I was gone so much I felt guilty leaving her.

When we reached the burger place, I found a seat at an outside table and tied Caper's leash to the leg of my chair. "I'll take the double cheeseburger meal."

"I'll be the one staying outside," Ann said. "I'll have the same."

The constant reminder of the danger irked me. I headed into the diner, placed our orders, and stood off to the side to wait until my name was called.

"You're the manager of Heavenly Acres, right?" A woman in her forties stepped beside me. "A lot of excitement around there. The lease on my apartment is up. Do you have any vacancies?"

"Several." I handed her a business card. "Call me to schedule a tour or look us up online."

"Thanks." She grabbed her tray from the counter and joined another woman in a booth. She said something to her, then they both glanced at me.

Forcing a smile, I picked up my order and hurried outside to Ann. "People are recognizing me and the news hasn't been on yet."

"I don't like that." Ann glanced at the window.

"Neither do I. Hopefully, she's what she says she is, which is a prospective tenant." I divided the food and held out a french fry to Caper.

While we ate, I filled Ann in on my theory. She sat back in her seat and quietly listened until I'd finished. "Well?" I took a bite of my burger.

"Interesting concept. Definitely warrants further research."

"Will you be calling your source?" I wiggled my eyebrows and made quote marks with my fingers.

"Yes." She ducked her head. "He can find out what isn't available to me."

"Ladies." Davis pulled up a chair, startling me. "Heard you wanted to talk." He glanced at me. "Over your snit?"

"Snit? Who talks that way anymore?" I grinned. "But yes, and I've been thinking."

"Oh, no." He stole one of my fries. To his credit, he also listened quietly.

The more I talked about my hunch, the more plausible it sounded. "Well?"

"I really wish you'd join the police academy and do all this investigating legally."

"I'm twenty-eight. Too old to start a new career. Besides, I hate running. What if I have to chase somebody down?"

He just gave me his look that told me I didn't warrant a response.

"Can we have a list of all crimes committed before and after I took over Heavenly Acres?"

"No."

"I can find out at the library."

"Then I guess you're going to the library." He stood.

"You think my idea is a good one." I grinned as he stole another fry.

"Maybe it's something I've already considered."

"Have you?"

He shrugged, giving me a shadow of a smile. "Be careful, CJ. Ann." He spun and strode to his car.

"He's wasting his words with that statement." Ann wadded up her napkin and tossed it on the tray. "Where to now?"

"Do we really have to go to the library or will your boyfriend make us a list?"

"He isn't my boyfriend."

"Whatever he is." *Boyfriend*. "We need as much information as he can get us." I stood. "Now, I need to have a long talk with my uncle." He had some explaining to do.

"How do you know he's home?"

I held up my phone. "Mags's tracker says she is. Larry is assigned to protect her."

Ann's eyes widened. "You don't have a tracker on me, do you?"

"Nope. That would be an invasion of privacy. Mags knows her phone has the app. She says it makes her feel safer." I tossed our garbage into the trashcan and unhooked Caper.

As we headed for the car, the two women from inside the diner watched us. I smiled and waved, only to have them turn their heads as if they hadn't seen me. I shrugged. I didn't have time to wonder why people acted strangely. I had a drug dealer to catch. Much better than the usual killer I got involved with, right?

Chapter Seven

Back at the house, I sat in an armchair across from where Larry and Mags reclined on the sofa watching a reality TV show. "We need to talk." I wiggled my finger back and forth between us. "You rented to your grandmother without letting me know. I'm either the manager or I'm not."

"You're the manager." Larry crossed his ankle over his knee. "Mom needed a place to live. She's gone through Dad's life insurance by online betting."

"She's living there free?"

He nodded. "I don't want her living with me. She's a bit...meddlesome. I'm sorry I didn't tell you."

"The secrecy hurts." I would not cry. I would not cry.

"I'm not used to having a family, CJ." He got up and knelt next to my chair. "For too many years I kept my personal life just that. Personal. Mags is helping me learn to let things out."

I glanced at my friend who gave a sharp nod.

"He's a real mess," she said.

"Okay." I sighed. "Why couldn't you have put your grandmother in house number ten? At least we know she wouldn't have been a murderer or thief." I still insisted that lot was cursed.

He laughed and stood. "Don't bet on it."

Ann came in the room after making a call in the kitchen. "We'll have a list by tonight."

"What kind of list?" Larry returned to the sofa.

"Of all the crimes committed in this area in the last year."

"You should know that," Mags said. "You've been involved in all of them."

My eyes widened. "I'm sure that isn't true."

She started ticking off on her fingers, ending with Robinson's death and the deer poaching. "The jewelry store heist happened in town, but the jewels ended up here. Need I say more? The woods and mountain around this area is perfect for bad guys to hide in, not to mention you're inexperienced. Anyone who cared to look would know the only job you'd had before was being a caregiver."

I glared. "Fine, but a list will tell us all the known people involved." Then I crossed my arms for effect. "And, I'm not inexperienced. I've helped catch killers."

"You know who all are involved, too."

I held up my hand when she held up hers. "Do not start counting again." Despite what she said, I still thought a list was a good idea.

Larry rubbed his chin. "A list would show us who is dead and who is incarcerated. We could visit the ones in prison and ask questions about anyone left on the outside who'd benefit from helping them. Will your contact be sharing that information?" He glanced at Ann.

"He'll give us everything he can find. I also know someone in prison who can help us with any incarcerated names."

My mind went back to the beginning—to the handsome, dirty cop behind the first thefts. Perk was dead, but his main squeeze, Addie Morris, was behind bars. "What do I have to do to pay Addie Morris a visit?"

"You have to be approved. It can take months," Larry said.

"I can get it done within a day." Ann typed into her phone. "But, I'll be going with you."

Could all that had happened really be traced back to one or a just few people? Could it be that easy? Hope leaped within me. Find the source, end the trouble, and get back to a normal life. I rubbed my hands together. Right.

"What's going through your head?" Mags studied me with narrowed eyes. "You're up to something."

"Of course, I am. I'm fighting for justice." I sprang up and headed for the bedroom to let Sherlock out.

"You've gone completely crazy," Mags called after me.

I opened the door. A meow drew my attention upward. Sherlock perched on the curtain rod, from which hung shredded sheers. "Cat, you're killing me." When I reached up to grab him, he Spidermanned down the curtains, pulling them free of the rod. Good thing I had blinds on the windows. The sheers had been purely decorative.

Sherlock streaked past me and out the door. Seconds later, Caper added her yelps to the chaos. I sat on my bed and fell backward, closing my eyes.

"I've got us an appointment to see Morris in the morning," Ann said from the doorway.

I opened one eye. "That's good. What should I wear?"

She rattled off several colors saying I couldn't wear what inmates or guards wore, no bare shoulders or cleavage, no shorts, and no underwire in my bra. "Certain jeans and shoes will set off the detector too, so bring a change of clothing. Best to stick to slacks and shirts that cover your shoulders and shoulder bones."

"My shoulder bones? What's sexy about those?"

She shrugged. "That's the rules."

"I need to go home and grab something."

"Let's go." She jerked her head.

I jumped to my feet, hunted down Sherlock who fought not be put back in my room. The little scamp would try to run out the front door if I didn't lock him up. Were there obedience classes for cats?

Kitten safely in my room, I followed Ann out to her car. "We're going to be going back and forth a lot."

"Yep." She slid into the driver's seat. "Can't be helped."

Neither could my thinking the more time we spent on the road, the easier it would be for someone to run us off said road and do away with us. I glanced over my shoulder. No one there.

"If you would have been this paranoid from day one," Ann said, "we wouldn't be in this mess."

"I'm not paranoid, just careful."

We pulled into Heavenly Acres to the sight of Roy refilling holes under the supervision of Mrs. Acres. My handyman did not look pleased.

"I wasn't aware Davis had the tape removed." I shoved open my door.

"I don't think he did."

An obvious look of relief crossed Roy's face when he joined us. "Save me."

I chuckled. "Who took down the tape?"

"I did." Mrs. Acres lifted her chin. "An absolute eyesore. I'm going to help you fill all these empty houses and lots. Flapping crime-scene tape will not help in that regard."

"It's a crime to remove the tape, ma'am." Ann's cop face slid into place.

"Oh, posh." The old woman waved a dismissive hand. "Who's going to arrest an old woman?"

Davis would, for sure. But then again, maybe not. I was still on this side of prison bars.

"I'll be wanting a sit-down conversation with you, too, Missy." She pointed at me. "That way we'll be on the same page as to what to do with this place."

"I've done a lot of things already, Mrs. Acres, but I welcome you to share your ideas." I'd manage to listen, then do what I thought was best. "I am the manager."

She rolled her eyes. "Only because my boy felt sorry for you."

I scowled. "That isn't true. It was to show his appreciation for caring for his mother." Why was I arguing with a bitter old woman? "A meeting will have to wait. I'm busy the next few days." I shot Roy an apologetic look. "You don't take orders from Mrs. Acres." I stormed to my house.

"She's going to make your life difficult," Ann said as I unlocked my front door.

"Yes, I believe she will." Another chat with Larry was in the near future. I climbed the stairs and grabbed a pair of yoga pants and a pair of slacks, then a tunic and a blouse I thought would be appropriate for a visit to the prison. From my window, I could see Eric was home. Good. A few minutes with him would brighten my day. I thundered down the stairs, tossed my clothes into the backseat of Ann's car, then rushed to see my guy.

He met me on his front porch, Hershey at his heels. "We were just on our way to your place." He smiled and wrapped his arms around me. "How does grilled steaks and salads sound?"

"For everyone? We've quite the crowd." I lifted my face for a kiss.

"Sure, I bought enough." He kissed me, slow and tender, then grabbed a large canvas bag from inside the door. "Want to ride with us? Ann can follow."

Ann opened her mouth to protest, then sighed instead. "Don't get too far ahead of me."

He laughed and led me to his jeep. Half an hour later, Grams's house was bursting at the seams. Rather than trip over each other, we took the dogs to the backyard, leaving the two cats to hiss at each other inside.

"You need to do something with your grandmother," I told Larry while Eric fired up the grill. "She removed the crime-scene tape illegally and is ordering Roy around. She also seems to think she can tell me what to do."

His eyes widened. "She's probably bored because she can't gamble anymore. I took over her finances and only give her an allowance. I'll talk to her."

"Talk to whom?" Mrs. Acres stepped through my backyard gate. "I do hope this snit of a girl isn't tattling on me."

Larry jumped to his feet fast enough to knock over his patio chair. "Grandma, how did you get here?"

"One of those paid-driver things. He's waiting in front for you to pay up." She lowered into the seat he'd righted. "Since Miss Turley left without speaking with me, I came here." She narrowed her eyes at me.

I arched a brow at Larry and jerked my head toward Mrs. Acres.

Taking a deep breath, he said, "You can't be bossing CJ or her staff around, Grandma. You are only a resident."

"I'm the grandmother of the man who owns the property, and don't anyone here forget that."

"As if you'd let us." Mags smirked.

Mrs. Acres whipped around to face her. Her gaze took in Mags's pink gym shoes and matching pants and shirt. "You look like cotton candy."

"Thank you." Mags grinned and set a large bowl of salad in the center of the patio table. "Do stay for supper, won't you? It'll be so much more pleasant."

I grinned. Mrs. Acres had met her match in Mags.

Larry looked stricken. "Uh, okay, uh, Grandma, this is my girlfriend, Mags Snyder."

"Girlfriend? What are you, thirteen?"

"Has she always been this sour?" Mags asked.

"Only since Gramps died. Can I get you a glass of water or tea, Grandma?"

"Tea."

"Lots of sugar," Mags said. "She needs sweetening up."

I choked back a laugh. "I'll get it." I jumped up, eager to step inside and away from the woman's acerbic wit. My heart ached a bit at knowing her attitude came because she missed her husband, but that didn't completely erase her rudeness.

I pulled two pitchers of tea from the fridge, one sweet, one non, and set them on a tray. I added glasses and a sugar jar in case what I made wasn't sweet enough. A dish of lemon slices and the tray was almost too heavy for me to carry.

Thankfully, Eric came in to grab the meat. "Here. Switch with me." He took the heavier tray, leaving me to carry the steaks. I followed him outside and set the plate of meat next to the grill, eyeing Hershey who salivated nearby.

"No." I made a stern face. "Do not touch."

"If you would've stuck around, Missy," Mrs. Acres said, "you would have seen the two men in cheap suits wandering through Heavenly Acres."

"Were they looking at houses?"

She shook her head, studying her nails. "No, they were more interested in the woods behind them. Wait, they did seem more than a little interested in your house."

"Did you talk to them?" My blood chilled.

"I told them you were living in town for a while."

Chapter Eight

The next morning, I still couldn't get over Mrs. Acres' loose lips. So much for hiding. It wouldn't be hard to find me now that the very ones I was hiding from knew where to look. "I might as well move back home."

"Safety in numbers," Ann said as we pulled onto the Interstate headed for the prison. "You might as well relax. We have a couple hours of driving."

"I can't believe how quickly that woman has butted into my life." I shifted in my seat to face Ann. "I don't like it."

She laughed. "I don't think the woman likes you either."

With a shrug, I turned back to the window and watched the trees zip by. It went against my grain not to like someone, but Larry's grandmother was surely testing me.

The closer we got to our destination, the more nervous I became. I'd never been in a prison before. I'd only seen them on the crime shows I loved to watch. They weren't welcoming places for visitors.

"Remove all jewelry and leave them in the car."

I nodded and removed my earrings. "Phone?"

She shook her head.

"Follow my example," Ann said as we walked toward the building. She pushed a button to open a gate leading to a tunnel of fencing and twisted barbed wire. When the gate closed, she pushed a button at the opposite end that led us into a room with guards, a German Shepherd, and a metal detector.

"Stand here, hands up," the guard holding the dog's leash told me after he'd finished with Ann.

I did as instructed, my heart in my throat, while the dog sniffed me. I almost fainted with relief when the man told me I was cleared. I showed my driver's license to the guard behind the desk and handed my shoes to the one on the other side of the metal detector.

Ann plopped a baggie full of coins on the desk with her driver's license and an unopened pack of cigarettes. "She'll be more willing to answer questions if we make her happy," she said.

Made sense to me. Ann led me to another door where a guard pushed a button. Once inside, after the door closed behind us, the door in front of us opened and we stepped into what looked like a school cafeteria where everyone wore uniforms of the same color. Ann told the guard there who we were visiting and were told to sit and wait.

We sat at a round table. Behind me were a line of vending machines and a shelf with games and books. It broke my heart to see children laughing and smiling while visiting an incarcerated mother.

Fifteen minutes later, Addie Morris, head high and eyes blazing, sauntered toward us. She plopped into a chair across from me. "You have a lot of nerve coming here."

"We'd like to ask you some questions," Ann said, sliding the pack of cigarettes to her.

"We have to go outside to smoke." Addie eyed the coins. "After we eat. I can't carry the coins. One of you has to go with me."

Ann stood. "CJ, do you want anything?"

"A diet soda and chips." Anything to keep me from staring at the people around me. I'd already gotten some stern looks.

When Ann and Addie returned, the table was full of junk food. Addie grinned and unwrapped a candy bar. "I'm not sure I'll get through all this before our time is up, but it isn't my money."

Ann's cop face slid into place. "Do you have anyone on the outside working for you?"

"In regard to what?" She took a bite of the candy.

"Cocaine, threats to CJ, lots of things." Ann sat back and crossed her arms.

Addie laughed. "Someone after your little pet again?"

"Me," I said, doing my best to adopt the persona of one of the investigators on the shows I enjoyed. I crossed my hands and leaned forward. "Since your arrest, Heavenly Acres and the campground have been plagued with crime. Know anything about it?"

"If I did, and I'm not saying I do, why tell you? You're the reason I'm locked up until I die."

"All the more reason to help us," Ann said. "I could put in a good word for you."

"And get me what, more time on the yard?" Addie rolled her eyes. "As far as I'm concerned, this little nosy mouse will get what she deserves." She glanced at the guard and lowered her voice. "Come outside with me. Leave the loot. No one will touch it." She snatched the cigarettes and shoved open a set of steel double doors.

Outside was more of a dog run in my opinion. A few canopies and picnic tables. An electric cigarette lighter.

Addie lit her cigarette. "Walk with me. Don't touch the fence. We'll get yelled at and draw attention."

Sounded sinister. Ann and I followed her to the furthest picnic table. "It isn't me running the show, ladies." She glared. "If anyone finds out I'm telling you this—"

"They won't." I acted startled by her fierce look. "You act angry at me, and I'll look threatened."

"Not too threatened or a guard will come over to investigate. I am angry at you."

"Why do crooks always act like the victim? If you hadn't tried to kill me, you wouldn't be in here and Perk wouldn't be dead."

"Don't say his name," she snarled. "Do you want the info or not?"

"We do." Ann put a restraining hand on my arm.

"The real kingpin is a man by the name of Dante Jacobson. Perk and I worked for him. In here it's his old lady, Clara, running things. People die in here, ladies. People who go against the Jacobsons don't see the sun rise the next day."

"Why Heavenly Acres?" I asked.

She moved to light another cigarette, then returned. "Another thing to blame you for. I didn't smoke until I got in here."

"Sorry." I repeated my question.

Ann glanced to where an African American woman came outside.

"Send drones up over that mountain. You'll see." She slapped her hands on the table. "Don't come see me again. I will not assuage your guilt for putting me here." She threw the cigarette on the ground, then picked it up when a guard blew her whistle.

When we returned inside, she was sitting at the table eating a bag of chips. The other woman also came back inside and sat at a table near us as if waiting for someone.

"I thought you wanted us to leave," I said.

"If you leave, I have to go back to my cell. You got two hours to sit there and watch me eat."

"Jacobson." The guard behind the desk stood. "Your visitor has left. Back to your cell."

My blood ran cold. Despite my attempt to act as if I'd never heard the name before, I got the feeling I failed.

Clara Jacobson's eyes narrowed. "Morris."

Addie cursed and lunged to her feet, squaring off with the other woman. "I can't help it if these two losers come in here giving me a hard time about nothing."

"Is that all it is?" Clara's gaze flicked to me and Ann.

"We tried to bribe info out of her," Ann said. "It's been a total waste of time." She motioned to the guard.

"No, I'm not finished eating."

Clara laughed. "You've got a cell full of food." She shook her head and headed for the door on the opposite side of the room.

"I'm dead." Addie shoved a cookie into her mouth. "Go now."

"I'll have a guard watch over you," Ann said.

"Twenty-four seven? Whatever." She joined Clara at the opposite end.

Ann scooped up the food and cigarettes. "Might as well put these in the cupboard at home."

We repeated the process to get out of the building. On the way to the car, Ann said, "It costs money on an inmate's account to purchase snacks. Who is funding Addie's?"

"Can your boyfriend find out?"

"He isn't my boyfriend."

"Whatever you say. Can he find out who is putting money on her books and who might work for the Jacobsons?"

She nodded. "I'll let Davis know what we discovered. He can get access to a drone or two."

"How long until whoever works for Dante and Clara find out we were here?"

"Before the end of the day. I guarantee you she'll be calling someone, and don't forget she had a visitor. I just didn't know who she was in order to pay attention."

Great. The danger to me had just tripled. The only place I'd be truly safe was Antarctica. Maybe.

Ann called Davis via Bluetooth once we were back on the road and told him of our visit with Addie. I could imagine the sternness on his face.

"Jacobson? Are you sure? He's been locked up for years," Davis said.

"If Clara Jacobson's reaction to seeing us with Addie is any indication, then yes," Ann replied.

"This just got a whole lot worse. Okay, I'll see what I can do about drones and keeping Morris alive." Click.

"You should go back on the police force."

"No, because then I have to follow the rules. I'm more useful as your bodyguard."

"Still just as bossy, though." I checked my phone to see if Mags was at her house or Grams's. Ann's house. "Head to Heavenly Acres. I'd like to see if we can catch a glimpse of the men in suits."

"Doesn't sound like gangsters."

"Mrs. Acres did say cheap suits." If they were wealthy gangsters, they'd wear suits. "I'd like to know why they acted interested in my house." When I started my job there, jewelry had been hidden under the floorboards. I'd been there long enough now to know nothing else was. The ground under my house was undisturbed other than the occasional hole Caper dug.

We found Mags at home, binoculars in hand, patrolling the edge of the tree line with a harried-looking Larry.

"Save me," he whispered.

"From what?" I grinned.

"My grandmother refuses to come out after what she says was unwelcome treatment last night, and Mags insists on walking back and forth in hopes of finding…something."

"How will we solve this case if we aren't actively

looking for that elusive something?" Mags tilted her head. "Tell him, CJ."

I told them about our visit to the prison. "I'd really like to know what the two men who were here yesterday looked like. Larry, will you go ask your grandmother?"

"She isn't talking to me."

"Who will she talk to?"

"Eric, and he's up the mountain."

My man could charm even the surliest woman. "Is he still tracking four-wheelers?"

Larry nodded. "He's getting frustrated. Said he's starting to feel as if he's being strung along as a joke."

I glanced at Ann. "What if that's exactly what's happening? What if whoever is behind this is keeping him away so he can't help us or find whatever is up there?"

"At least they haven't run him off the road," Mags said. "Better to waste time in a beautiful forest."

I whipped to face her. "He's in danger. If he's starting to realize the tracks mean nothing, he'll start looking elsewhere. If he stumbles across whatever it is, they'll kill him. Remember the drug crop a few months ago? I almost died."

I marched to house number twenty and knocked on the door. When Mrs. Acres answered, I politely asked for the men's descriptions. "I've had enough of people arguing with me today, ma'am, so I'd appreciate your cooperation. You were not snubbed last night. If you were, I offer my most sincere apologies." I gave a smart-aleck bow.

"Impertinent. Here." She thrust her cell phone at me. "I snapped their picture."

I opened her photo gallery and stared at two men, one African, one white. "You, Mrs. Acres, are marvelous."

"It's about time you realized that."

I sent the photos to my phone and handed hers back to her. "Be careful. You don't want to get involved in the stuff I get into."

"I just might, Missy. Life is boring at my age."

Chapter Nine

"I should have put her in assisted living," Larry said when I told him of his grandmother taking photos.

"Hush, dear." Mags patted his hand. "It might be a good thing. No one would suspect an old woman of meddling."

Ann and I exchanged an amused glance. Mags was quickly approaching the threshold of old age, and she was the biggest meddler I knew.

Ann sprang to her feet at a knock on the door. She peered out the peephole. "It's Eric." Opening the door, she stepped back to let him and Hershey in. The chocolate lab made a beeline for my bedroom, no doubt to terrorize Sherlock.

After a quick kiss, Eric fell onto the sofa next to me. "I'm worn out."

"No doubt," Larry said. "We've determined—guessed actually—that you're being led on a wild goose chase to keep you away from Heavenly Acres and/or the campground. With you gone and CJ here, the bad guys can do anything they want."

"Except for your grandmother," Mags reminded him. "I'll make some spaghetti and garlic toast. How does that sound?"

"Wonderful." I smiled. "I'll whip up a salad in a bit." At the moment, I wanted to be with Eric but realized I shouldn't let Mags have to do all the supper preparations. I'd cuddle with my man later. "Do you want a cup of coffee?"

"That would be wonderful." He smiled and lifted my hand to his lips.

Grinning, I got to my feet. "I'll be right back." In the kitchen, I made his coffee, delivered it, then returned to make the salad.

Mags snapped spaghetti pasta in half and dropped them into a pan of boiling water. "Larry's right. Mrs. Acres shouldn't be there alone."

My eyes widened. "You aren't considering moving her here with us, are you? Where would we put her?" Besides, the house wasn't big enough for someone with such a sour disposition.

Mags shuddered. "With me."

"Don't be a martyr." Now that the idea was out there, I couldn't think of anything else. "I don't like all the targets under the same roof."

"Sitting ducks." She nodded. "If someone wanted to blow up the house, we'd all be gone at once. Ann doesn't like it, either. I can see it in her eyes."

"But going home would separate us so we could be picked off one-by-one. There isn't a foolproof way. Eric's still in his house and no one has come after him."

"Larry told me about your visit to the prison." Eric came up behind me and wrapped his arms around my waist. "And, just because no one has tried anything yet doesn't mean they won't. Hershey is a great alarm system."

I turned and lifted my gaze to his. "Caper is, too."

"But people aren't afraid of ankle biters." He smiled.

"No one has tried to hurt me or threaten me."

"They will now. You've been caught by Clara Jacobson."

"In the past, we've had a dead body by now." I really was beginning to think the danger wasn't to me. The bad guys just wanted their drugs.

"Let's keep it that way. We don't want you to be the first." He kissed the top of my head and returned to the living room.

"We need to see where those three men were executed and try retracing their steps," Mags said in a low voice. "If we all have to live crammed in this house much longer, I might be the one shooting someone."

"Especially if Mrs. Acres moves in." I grinned and placed the salad in the center of the dining-room table.

"I might shoot myself in that case." She set the spaghetti on the table and went to get the bread. "Supper."

"We're right here," Ann said with a frown. "No need to yell. I seriously need some privacy and quiet."

"Maybe you should spend some time in the chapel tomorrow," I suggested. "It always helps me."

My cell phone rang as we sat down to eat. I excused myself and quickly answered. "Hello?"

"Is this CJ Turkey? We met at the burger place when I asked about a rental."

"Oh, yes. I remember you."

"Is it possible to check one out in the morning around nine o'clock?"

"Sure thing. I'll meet you at house number one at nine." I hung up and returned to the table. "A prospective tenant."

"So much for the chapel." Ann twirled her fork in her plate of pasta.

"We can go before or after." I reached down and peeled Sherlock from my leg. How old did a cat have to be before you could declaw them?

The next morning, Ann and I arrived at my house by eight-thirty. Tears clogged my throat when I glanced at the picnic table where I'd started so many mornings having coffee with Eric. Many nights we'd sit there and watch the moon sparkle on the lake. Someday I hoped we could do so again.

Ann entered my house, returning outside after a couple of minutes. "Looks clear."

"There isn't a lot of places for someone to hide." I hefted a bag of dirty laundry over my shoulder. I might as well do some wash while we were here. The washer at Grams's house was always occupied it seemed.

By the time I'd started the small load, a car pulled up outside. Ann appeared at my side to greet the woman from the burger place.

"I'm Carla Jennings," she said, offering her hand. "I'm very excited."

"Wonderful." I smiled. "Let me show you house number eight."

Number eight was a white house with deep green trim. "It's 270 square feet of absolute cuteness." I unlocked the door to a furnished Cape Cod-style tiny house. White and pale wood everywhere the eyes landed.

"It's adorable." Carla clapped her hands. "I'll take it. Can I move in today?"

"Sure. Follow me back to my house to sign the lease. How long will you be staying?"

"I'm not sure yet. Will that be a problem?"

I shook my head. "We have other vacancies." Not that I was expecting a rush anytime soon. Sad, really. Last spring the place was full. I told her about the chapel, the hiking trails, and which part of the lake was safe for swimming. "Curfew is ten o'clock on weeknights, midnight on the weekend. Now that the weather is nice again, we'll be having monthly community get-togethers. I think you'll like it here." I motioned for her to sit at the outside table while I went into my house to get a lease.

Soon, I'd taken first and last month's rent and waved at my newest tenant who drove away saying she'd return shortly with her personal things.

"Chapel?" I glanced at Ann.

"Most definitely."

At the chapel, I sat on the front pew on one side, Ann on the other. I guess she really did seek some solitude. The peace of the place immediately filled me. While we didn't have a pastor who gave messages here, God's presence was definitely in that small, glass-walled building. I glanced toward the lake where the giant cross illuminated every night. I smiled, thinking of the time it had literally saved my life.

I'd been chased through the dark by a killer, whom I then blinded by the light of the cross that I suddenly turned on. Since then, I had the cross on a timer to come on every night rain or shine.

I wasn't sure how long we sat there before Ann stood. "I'm good," she said, "and I have a plan."

"Do you want to share it?"

"Sure." She sat next to me. "My contact—"

"Boyfriend."

"Stop it. My contact sent me the list of all known associates of the Jacobsons. Some of them we have photos of, others we don't. Same with home and work addresses. It's a place to start."

"Mags wants to go to where the pretend grounds-crew men were killed and move backward."

Ann thought for a minute, then nodded. "Sounds good. Ready?"

"I need to do some things at the house first." Like clean the expired food out of the fridge and gather my clean laundry. It wouldn't take long, but it would give me a feeling of normalcy, something I craved.

Mags must have had the same thought because she puttered in her flower bed when we arrived at my house. A watchful Larry read a book on the tiny front porch. He gave a welcoming nod, then returned to his book.

I smiled and entered my house. A few slices of bread and some lunchmeat were still good, so rather than throw them out, I made Ann and me sandwiches for lunch. A few other things went in the garbage to be taken to the dumpster on our way back to town.

I glanced out the window to see a large motorhome pull into the campgrounds and hook up to one of the sites. Maybe things were returning to normal after all. I'd place an ad in the local newspaper for Heavenly Acres and make it sound as if folks needed to act fast or miss out.

By the time I'd carried the sandwiches outside to Ann, she'd placed the printed lists from her boyfriend/contact on the table. "We aren't dealing with only men, as I'm sure you're aware," she said. "Nor are we dealing with one ethnic group. The Jacobsons' arms are far-reaching, even into Missouri, Texas, and Louisiana."

"What are they involved in?"

"Trafficking, drugs, dealing arms—you name it, they're doing it, or someone is doing it for them. Both Clara and Dante have over twenty thousand dollars on their commissary accounts. They aren't hurting too bad."

"Where does the rest of the money from their operations go?"

"Offshore, I bet." Ann rolled her head on her shoulders. "Someone is making a pretty penny for them, and it's not the two guys in cheap suits Mrs. Acres saw. They'd be flaunting their wealth."

"Anyone like that in town?" I bit into my ham and cheese.

"Warrants looking into, but I'm guessing a nearby larger city."

"Something else for your contact." I made finger quotes. "To check into."

"Stop it." She ducked her head to hide a grin.

I laughed and followed Carla Jennings' car as it drove past and parked in front of number eight. "That didn't take long." She opened her car trunk and hefted out two suitcases. The back seat was piled with boxes. "I hope she realizes there isn't a lot of space in a tiny house for possessions."

Across the green area, Mrs. Acres stepped out of her house and openly stared at Carla as she carried her things inside. I didn't think Heavenly Acres could handle two nosy people. The residents might rebel.

"Make her stop." Rose Flower rushed toward us.

"Who?" I frowned.

"The old woman. She's always watching. Danny almost kissed me last night. He would have too, if she hadn't been wagging her finger at us." Rose crossed her arms. "She's mean to my brothers and yells whenever they get too close to her property."

"They shouldn't be on her property," Ann said. "Not that there's much to get on."

"Briar is looking for more bags so he has to go everywhere. Some man said he'd pay him twenty dollars for every one he found."

Chapter Ten

"Bring Briar to me." Ann's cop face replaced her more friendly one.

"Are you going to arrest him?" Rose paled.

"Don't be ridiculous. Bring him. Now."

The girl ran off. I couldn't help but laugh, despite the seriousness of someone using a small child to dig up cocaine. Oh, to be sixteen again and irate over a missed opportunity for a kiss.

"It isn't funny." Ann frowned. "Those children are in danger."

"I'm not laughing at that. Poor Rose." I snorted in my attempt to stifle my laughter.

Ann's mouth twitched. "It is cute."

Briar's mother, Lucy, looked anything but happy as she followed her son across the road. "What's he done now?" She asked. "You know you can't question someone's child without a parent present."

"Please have a seat, Lucy. This is important." I motioned for her to sit next to me.

"Briar, is it true someone asked you to find more

bags and that same someone will pay you twenty dollars?" Ann pulled a small notepad and pencil from her bag.

"What?" Lucy gasped, gripping her son's arm. "I thought you were smarter than that, son. You're ten, not two. Don't you realize there's drugs in those bags? That the man offering you that money is a bad guy?" She glanced at Ann. "I don't know what to do with these kids."

"The most important thing right now is to keep them safe," I said. "Briar, tell Ann what the man looks like."

"Am I in trouble?"

Ann shook her head. "Just describe him, please."

"He's about the same size as Mom's boyfriend, Dave, except he has black hair and brown skin. Really white teeth, and he has a big gold ring on his finger."

"That's an amazing description," Ann said. "You are a very observant young man."

Briar puffed out his chest. "I like cop shows."

"Me too." I held up my hand for a high-five, then grinned at Ann. "See? Those shows are educational."

"Whatever. Do you remember anything else? Have you found any bags and received money?"

"Not yet." His smile faded, replaced by a furrowed brow. "He told me not to tell anyone. Now Rose and y'all know. I need Witness Protection."

"For crying out loud." Lucy lunged to her feet. "We're going to stay with my mother for a while. Maybe she can knock some sense into my children's thick heads." Her face darkened. "Now, you'll have to change schools, make new friends—"

"Not for real!" Tears welled in Briar's eyes. "Rose is going to kill me. She's in love with Danny."

"Dear God, spare me." Lucy took a firm hold of his arm. "It's only for the last few months of school. Hopefully by then, the bad guys will be locked up. Are we finished here?" She scribbled a phone number on Ann's pad. "You can reach me there."

"Yes, ma'am." Ann closed her notebook and stared at Briar. "Don't give your mother trouble. You brought this on yourself by associating with someone you didn't know. Someone who offered you money to do something you knew was wrong. Do you understand?"

"Yes, ma'am." He glanced at me. "Are you sure she isn't still a cop?"

"I'm sure." I grinned. "All this will be over soon." I wanted to make him a promise but knew it might not be one I could keep. "I guess we call Davis now?"

"Yep. He'll have his own questions for Briar." She sighed and placed the call.

I could hear Davis yelling through the phone. He wasn't happy she'd questioned the boy without him.

"I didn't want to delay his mother taking her family to safety. I'll text you the phone number she left." Ann hung up and sent the text. "If I was on the force, I'd have been suspended. That's why I don't want to be a police officer anymore."

"We'll be lucky if we get through this without being arrested." Davis could only be pushed so far and I felt as if Ann and I were teetering on the brink. "Briar's description won't help us find this man through your contact's database, will it?"

"No. All we can do is be on the lookout."

Mags pulled up next to us in her car. "Let's go before Larry gets back."

"Where is he?" Ann glanced around. "He's your guard."

"Scoping the perimeter. We heard about Briar. His mother was screaming loud enough to be heard in the next county. Come on." She raised her eyebrows. "There's an alley waiting for us."

"We should wait," Ann said.

"I'll go alone." Mags gave a sinister smile. "I need a break from Larry, bless his heart."

"We planned on going anyway." I glanced at Ann.

"Fine." She opened the driver-side door. "I'll drive."

"You don't trust my driving?" Mags glowered.

"Nope. My car." Leaving the door open, she climbed into her car.

I gave Mags a shrug and chose the front passenger seat, leaving the back for Mags. "I thought you were in a hurry."

She grabbed her purse and darted toward us as Larry drove up on a golf cart. "Go." She dove in and slammed the door before blowing Larry a kiss. "See you later, sweetie."

"Hey." He raced after us as far as the entrance, then stopped. I had no doubt he'd be placing a call to Davis, Eric, or both. Yep. I could see jail time in the near future.

"Have either of you ever been arrested?" I asked. Grams would roll over in her grave.

"Oh, sure. Several times," Mags said. "I used to

protest just about anything when I was younger. It wasn't so bad. You meet all kinds of interesting people."

Ann pressed her lips together but couldn't hide the smile. "I have to admit I've missed the three of us getting into trouble."

Mags slapped the back of the seat. "Let's go catch a bad guy."

If only it were that easy. Ann drove to a vacant warehouse on the edge of town. The area might have been prosperous once, but now corner stores and empty storefronts mingled with pawn shops. I didn't hold out much hope of finding a clue.

"We should have brought that nosy dog of yours, CJ," Mags said. "She always finds something. There isn't much here other than garbage."

Which is exactly why my dog shouldn't be here. She might bring up a body part. It wouldn't be the first time.

I got out of the car and stood in the middle of the lot. "Where did it happen?"

Ann glanced at her phone. "Behind the building." She set out in that direction, glancing back when Mags hesitated. "Come on. This was your idea. The bodies are long gone."

"I hope so." She shoved her hands into the pockets of her bright orange capris.

"You were gung-ho when we left. What happened?" I asked.

"I regained my sense."

"Ha." Ann said. "The day that happens is the day CJ's dog flies."

"Why does everyone pick on my poor pooch?" I

glanced from one to the other. "Let's settle on the task at hand, then start asking some questions of the few shops that are open."

"Who made you the boss?" Mags stopped and peered at something on the ground. "Is that blood?"

Ann glanced down. "More like oil. The men weren't killed here in the open."

"There's an awful lot of oil."

"Trucks were parked here. They sometimes leak." Ann shook her head.

"Okay."

Ann stopped at the corner of the building and peeked around the corner. "All clear."

What exactly did she think she'd see? I took a deep breath to steady my nerves, guessing Mags's nervousness had rubbed off, and followed Ann into a narrow space between the building and a concrete-block wall. The only thing back there were a dumpster and stains on the wall, of which I didn't want to contemplate their origin.

"Gross." Mags, of course, moved in for a closer look. "Yep. People were killed here. Look. Bullet holes." She pointed at the wall. "Now what?"

Ann rolled her eyes. "We know they were killed here. We're looking for something we don't already know."

"CJ, climb in the dumpster. You always find something when you go digging." Mags motioned her head.

"Why don't you?" I frowned.

"These are new pants."

"Fine." Knowing I'd regret the act, I pulled a concrete block over and stepped up. Thankfully, the dumpster was empty. "Dead end. Let's go talk to someone."

The sun went behind a cloud making the alley even more sinister. A breeze kicked up, blowing a sheet of paper across the cracked asphalt. We were wasting time.

"Bingo." Ann stood from where she squatted near a fence. "A footprint. It looks like the same print as the one found outside Mags's house. Someone was careless when they removed the bodies."

My eyes widened. "Didn't the coroner's office move them?"

"Yep."

"That means—"

Mags clapped her hands. "Our first clue."

"Our first solid one, anyway." Ann grinned. "Let's go talk to some people."

Our first stop was the pawn shop. Ann showed the man her identification while Mags browsed the shelves.

"Do you know anything about the three murders that took place here a few months back?" Ann asked.

"Look, ladies. I don't want any trouble. Talking around here gets folks dead."

"We aren't cops," Mags said. "Someone is threatening us, and we want them to stop."

"Why you?"

"Because my friend here is nosy." She jerked her thumb toward me.

Seriously? It was a tossup in my opinion.

"It happened at night. I was closed."

"Do you have CCTV cameras?

"Yeah." He clearly hated admitting to that.

"How much is this gun?" Mags pointed to a pink handled Glock.

"Six hundred."

Ann sighed. "Focus. May we see the film?"

"Nothing to see. Three men walking across the lot holding guns on three more men." He pulled a laptop from under the counter. "You can't see their faces." He punched a code into the keyboard.

"Why didn't you hand this over to the police?" Ann's eyes narrowed.

"I don't like cops. They're always hassling me about selling stolen goods." He turned the laptop so we could see.

The pawnshop might be on the corner, but the lot was still too far away to gather many details other than it looked like two Hispanic men and one Caucasian walking behind three other men who wore hoods. One of them tripped, only to get a kick for his effort before being hauled back to his feet.

"I want this gun," Mags said. "Do you take checks?"

"You do not need a gun," Ann said. "The world does not want you armed. You do enough damage with your Taser." She glanced at the shop owner. "Do not sell it to her."

Mags scowled. "You'll regret that when those three men come after us. My hunting rifle won't be much help. Hey, do you have an automatic—"

Ann closed her eyes. Her lips moved in either a prayer or a count to ten. When she opened them, she thanked the shop owner and took Mags by the arm. "Time to move on."

Our next stop was a convenience mart whose

cameras had a better view of the lot but weren't working. The gal behind the counter worked days but said the man who worked nights hadn't talked about anything else but the shootings for weeks.

She leaned her elbows on the counter. "Marco said he thought the store was being robbed and ducked down here so he wouldn't get shot."

"So he didn't see anything?" I asked.

"Not really. Three shots. He ducked down after the first one. Then when no more came after the third shot, he stood in time to see a big black Cadillac drive by. He's pretty certain the men who killed the other ones were driving."

"Did he get the license plate number?" Hope leaped, only to be dashed when she shook her head. "But he recognized the driver. Said he goes to the bar on Second Street a lot. Big white smile, flashy ring."

Chapter Eleven

We glanced at one another and rushed out the door. I tossed a "thank you" over my shoulder.

Two seconds later, we stood on the sidewalk and stared at Ann's car. The tires and hubcaps were gone, the windows shattered.

"I hope you didn't have anything valuable in there," Mags said. "I also hope you have good insurance."

"Nope, because of the possibility of this, and my insurance is great. I'm on the seedy side of town too often to skimp on those things." Ann moved to the trunk where someone had tried unsuccessfully to pry it open. "I also installed a lock here in case I do need to leave something."

"Looks like we're walking to the bar." Too bad. It had to be at least four blocks. "Then we can call for someone to come get us." Otherwise, our quest would be interrupted, and we were on a roll.

Walking was a bad idea. Groups of scary-looking youth hung out on street corners. They jeered and made obscene gestures as we passed. I did my best to look purposeful. Sweat trickled down my spine.

"I'd like to zap the sneer off their faces." Mags snarled at one who ventured too close.

"Do not do that," Ann said sharply. "I'd like to make it until tomorrow alive."

She wasn't the only one. I bit back a yelp when a young man fell into step next to me and made kissy sounds. It didn't take long for me to realize he was speaking between the lip smacks. "Watch your back. Jose is watching." He fell back with the others.

I glanced over my shoulder. The boy gave a sharp nod. We now had a name. Hopefully, it was the right name.

"What did he say to you?" Ann's voice was barely above a whisper.

"He gave me the name of Jose." I was hoping the man with the big smile and flashy ring would be the owner of that name.

"CJ's the pretty one," Mags said. "She should flirt with the guy."

I glanced down at my denim capris and modest tee-shirt. "I don't really look the part."

"It won't be necessary. If our guy is in there, he already knows we're coming." Ann opened the worn wooden door.

The inside of the bar was dimly lit and had more patrons then I would've expected for the middle of the afternoon. Not even suppertime yet and every barstool held somebody. Most of the tables had at least one person sitting there nursing a drink.

The bartender, a big muscled man, narrowed his eyes at us when we entered. I could feel his gaze on my back as we walked into the room.

In the corner sat a big Hispanic man. I didn't know if his teeth were whitened, but he was wearing a large gold ring. I squared my shoulders and led the other two to his table. Not waiting for an invitation to sit, I pulled out a chair, sat, and smiled. "Hello, Jose."

His grin could've blinded me. "You've been busy, little girl. Have your guard dogs step back. I'll only talk to you."

"Did you have my friend's car vandalized?" I folded my hands on the fake wood grain of the Formica tabletop.

"No, but any of the gangs would help themselves when they saw a car full of white women pull up. You've been asking questions, going where you shouldn't—"

"Are you responsible for those three men's deaths?"

"What three men?" His smile didn't fade and he arched a brow.

"Why don't you tell me about all the cocaine being found, and why you enlisted the help of a ten-year-old boy?"

"I'm not quite sure what you're talking about." He drummed his fingers. "I have men on my payroll. Why would I need a child?"

I shrugged. "That's the million-dollar question. Maybe you can answer this one. Why me? Why Heavenly Acres?"

"It's nothing personal, little girl. What's been going on is the same as what's been going on for a hundred years."

"Which is?"

"The search for riches." He sat back in his chair. "Look. I like you, and I'd rather you not get yourself killed. Why not take a vacation? A nice long one."

"That sounds like a threat."

"Not at all. Think of it as a suggestion."

We had an old-fashioned stare-down for several seconds before a pretty server in black slacks and a white shirt slipped Jose a folded sheet of paper. He opened it, read it, and said, "I'm afraid your time is over."

I hoped he meant the conversation was over. "Thank you for your time." I stood and, without glancing back, marched outside.

When we reached the spot where we'd left Ann's car, the spot was empty.

"Got towed," a young black man said, handing Ann a business card. "Can't leave junkers lying around. Messes up the ambiance." He laughed and ran to join his friends.

"We are definitely being ganged up on," Mags said. "Let me call Larry to come and get us." Maybe you two could look around and find us a safe place to hole up until he gets here."

"The only place I see is that hole-in-the-wall Mexican food place across the street." I motioned to a restaurant, and wouldn't you know? It was called Jose's. "Tell Larry to pick us up there."

She placed the call, rolling her eyes as he scolded her, then we hurried across the street and into the restaurant. A sign announced for us to seat ourselves. We chose a table near the door where Ann could see everyone coming and going.

The waitress set a bowl of chips and another of salsa in front of us, then handed us menus. "Welcome to Jose's."

"Thank you," I smiled, not sure whether she had any affiliation with the big man we'd just left and figured it best to be as friendly as possible. After we'd placed our order, I said to the others, "I think we know who is standing in for the Jacobsons."

"Yes, but we didn't get much more than that." Ann shook her head.

"Don't forget the mention of treasure." Mags dipped a chip in the salsa. "That would explain all the crime. Everyone wants a piece."

Ann blinked several times, then sighed. "I don't think he meant a literal treasure, only that crooks have been using that mountain for a long time and don't see any reason to stop now."

"Too bad Larry didn't know that before he bought those huge parcels of land," Mags said.

"He owns more than one?"

She nodded. "The campground is government land, so he couldn't purchase it. With the success of Heavenly Acres, he's thinking about building another community further up the mountain."

A throbbing started at my temple. "That's it."

"What?" Mags reached for another chip.

They're causing problems at Heavenly Acres to prevent Larry from building on his other land. When was the last time he was up there?"

"I don't know. We've just been talking." A line appeared between her brows. "You think the treasure is on his land?"

"I think the treasure *is* his land," Ann said. "It's

the last boundary before whatever those people have been up to for so long is discovered. I need to find out what's happening with the drones." Ann pulled out her phone and typed on the screen. She received an almost immediate reply. "John says…crap." She closed her eyes and counted.

"So, his name is John." I grinned. "What does John say?"

"Don't tell anyone he's my source, please. He says the FBI has taken over the case and they've sent up drones that reveal nothing."

"It's heavily wooded. Maybe whatever is up there is camouflaged." We needed an aerial map and one of the terrain. A bit of history and what used to be up there.

"Maybe it's a diamond mine," Mags suggested. "Arkansas has lots of diamonds."

Ann's forehead wrinkled. "We're getting closer. What if there are tunnels in that mountain?"

"Ones that provides easy moving back and forth between destinations?" I asked.

"Yes. Ones that could also hide illegal activities. That could be the treasure. There's bound to have been a lot of moonshine being moved around here during Prohibition."

I wanted to clap my hands. We were figuring things out and hadn't had any real danger happen to any of us yet. "We're getting good at this."

The waitress brought our orders at the same time Larry arrived. He slid into the booth next to Ann and asked the waitress for enchiladas, also placing a to-go order for Eric. "Davis is fit to be tied," he said. "Not that I was in a good mood to be left behind."

Mags reached across the table and put her hand over his. "Sweetheart, you would've ruined everything." She filled him in on all that we'd discovered.

"Tunnels?" His eyes widened. "I'll see if I can't find a map or something. Good job, ladies."

"Are we forgiven?" Mags batted her lashes.

"Not by a long shot." His tender smile said otherwise.

I missed my man. I pulled out my phone to see where he was. The campgrounds. "Let's eat and get home. I'd like to spend more time with Eric than a couple of hours during suppertime."

"We need to see about my car," Ann said.

"It isn't drivable. You'll need tires first."

"Relegated to either Mags's big car or the Prius. Ugh."

"There's nothing wrong with my car." I stabbed my chimichanga hard enough for the fork to ding the plate.

"It won't go fast enough if someone is chasing us."

"Then I guess you need to get yours fixed."

"You ladies seem a bit testy today." Larry glanced from one to the other.

"It's been a long day," I said. "I'm sorry, Ann. This isn't like me."

"I know." She flashed a grin.

We waited while Larry ate, then had him drive us to Heavenly Acres so I could see Eric and get my car. Larry said he'd take Mags back to the house and see us later.

Ann and I climbed into the golf cart and sped

around the lake to where Eric was walking around the campsites.

He glanced up. "Hey."

"Hey," I said. "Looking for something?"

"One of the day campers lost a ring. She said she'd walked along the circle before noticing it gone. I doubt I'll find it but thought I'd try."

"That's my man. Always helping others."

"What have you two been up to? Larry and Davis were both texting me as if I could stop you from doing whatever it was you were doing."

I told him about our day. His expression flitted from interest, to a flash of anger, to worry, to intrigue. "Wow. You've managed to do more in one day than our local police."

"The local station needs more officers," Ann said. "No, I won't reenlist."

"The FBI are here now, anyway. I'm sure Davis is filling them in on everyone involved," Eric said, his gaze going to the Styrofoam container on the golf cart seat. "Is that my food?"

"I'm sorry. It's probably cold." I retrieved the box and handed it to him.

"I'm heading home and will nuke it. No big deal. Follow me over?"

I nodded and returned to the cart. Eric's rig was a lot faster than mine, giving me a bit of cart envy. Maybe I could get Larry to okay a Gator for me. Not that I needed one to putter around the community. I stopped the cart and climbed out as a black SUV pulled up alongside us. Davis, along with two men in black suits and dark sunglasses, stepped out. FBI, I figured from the cliched look.

"Clarice Josephine Turley?" One said. The other named Ann.

Davis, the traitor, said, "You two are under arrest for interfering in a police investigation."

Chapter Twelve

"Aren't you going to introduce me to your friends, Detective?" I spat out his title from the backseat of the SUV and did my best not to look into Eric's startled face.

Ann bumped her knee against mine and sent me a warning look. Her brows knit together. "Don't make it worse," she whispered.

"Agent Gavin and Agent Thompson, meet two of the three thorns in my side." Davis sat in the back with us, eyes straight ahead, not acknowledging us with even a glance.

"Did you arrest Mags, too?" I'm pretty sure my eyebrows disappeared into my hairline.

No answer, which told me yes, they'd arrested Mags, too. Poor Milton. He'd have been the one sent since Ann and I had the pleasure of these three. They must have thought we'd be difficult. At least we weren't handcuffed.

At the police station we were led to the one-and-only interrogation room, read our rights for the second time, and told to sit down. We sat.

The FBI agents left, leaving Davis to talk to us. His folded arms rested on the stainless-steel table. "You can't say I didn't warn you."

"Why aren't the FBI questioning us?" Ann asked, her eyes stormy.

"They don't want to be bothered but told me I needed to do something about the three stooges before they got themselves killed." His gaze flicked to what I knew to be a two-way mirror. Ah, they were watching us.

"Can we be released on bail?" Ann lifted her chin.

"In the morning. We're serious about you staying out of things." His gaze locked on mine. A question flickered there. He wanted to know what we'd found out the day before but couldn't ask.

I gave a subtle shake of my head. I wouldn't talk with the agents listening. What if they made things worse and the bad guys took off before we could catch them? Or what if they kept us from getting those maps? *Please, say you didn't arrest Larry.* Hopefully, Larry was doing what we'd discussed before the FBI put a stop to our plan. "What now?" I tilted my head.

"You'll be fingerprinted and put in a cell for the night." Davis stood. "I'm sorry, but I warned you over and over. Will you come peacefully?"

I rolled my eyes. "Of course."

He led us to a small room where we turned over our personal possessions, signed a paper listing them, and were fingerprinted. After that, we were led to a cell with two other women and a grinning Mags.

"This has been the most adventurous day," she said when Davis unlocked the cell door.

Ann put a finger to her lips.

"Right." Mags pretended to lock her lips.

Sadness clouded Davis's face as he locked the door behind us. "We'll bring you something to eat in a bit."

Two women in their thirties, stocky, and tough-looking with short hair and sleeveless tee-shirts glared at Ann. One of them said, "Look who is now one of us."

"Hello, Jean." Ann sat on the bench next to Mags. "Still selling drugs?"

"Nah. This time I'm in for breaking and entering my ex's place. Got caught before I could do any real damage. Lou, here—" She jerked her thumb toward the other woman, "was acting as my lookout. She wasn't very good."

"I just stepped around the corner to have a smoke," Lou said. "I didn't expect the chubby cop to drive by with this lady in the backseat." She motioned at Mags.

"Yep. He'd already nabbed me before catching you." Mags straightened and looked quite proud of herself.

"What are you two in for?" Jean asked.

"Same as Mags," I said. "Interfering in a police investigation."

"I know you. You're the one who keeps bringing down the hard-core criminals in this town." Awe crossed Jean's face. "I expected you to look tougher."

"A small stature and bright mind are my greatest

assets." I grinned.

"This isn't a party." Ann frowned. "You now have a police record."

"Lighten up," Mags said. "It's trump charges, and you know it. We'll be out of here in the morning, so you might as well enjoy the slumber party."

"What were y'all meddling in?" Lou asked. "Anything we've heard of?"

"We were asking questions about Jose." Mag's chest puffed up. "That's how tough we are."

"That man is bad news." Jean lowered her voice and leaned closer. "You know who he's standing in for, right?"

I nodded. "Jacobson." Which reminded me I needed to ask Davis whether Addie was safe.

"That husband-and-wife team have long arms. You might want to ask if you can stay locked up in here."

"For how long?" I arched a brow. "Crime has been going on for a long time. They've had their hairy fingers in everything, even poaching. I want it to be over."

"It'll be over if you get killed."

True. I rested my head against the cement-block wall behind me, suddenly overcome with exhaustion. I wouldn't have called the day an adventure as Mags had, but it was definitely eventful. I hoped Eric would bail me out in the morning and Larry would take care of the pets.

Supper that night was pasta and garlic bread from a local restaurant delivered by Milton. He slid a tray with five Styrofoam containers and five take-out cups full of tears under a pass-through in the door.

His gaze met mine and he shook his head. "Hate seeing you lowered to this."

"I wouldn't be in here if the FBI hadn't been called." I passed out the containers.

"We didn't call them. They showed up because of all the crime and overheard me and Davis talking about you three. They immediately wanted you out of the picture."

"Are we sure they're FBI?"

He nodded. "Identification shown and confirmed."

I guess it was just a matter of time before they showed up. "They're going to scare the bad guys away, and we'll never get this wrapped up."

"You'll still be alive, CJ." Milton heaved a sigh and left us, promising to return later to pick up the empty containers.

"He's right," Ann said.

"I thought you wanted to stop all this as much as I do."

"I do. I'm just saying it's going to be dangerous."

"We might die," Mags added.

"You two are free to back out."

"No. Carla Jacobson knows we're asking questions. Jose will have told Dante. We're in it to the end." Ann opened her container and made a face. "Noodles aren't very *al dente*."

"You can't be choosy in the slammer." Mags dug in.

Since I've always had a healthy appetite, despite being petite, I ate with gusto. The tea would hopefully help keep me awake. I'd seen way too many shows where someone fell asleep behind bars and had their throat slit. Jean and Lou seemed nice enough, but I wasn't taking any chances

I fell asleep and woke to complete darkness and a crick in my neck. Groaning, I pushed to my feet and paced the cell, waving my arms to get my circulation going. I paused at the door, hearing voices. It didn't take long to determine I was eavesdropping on the FBI agents.

"Detective Davis says she ought to be a police officer," one of them said.

I smiled. They had to be talking about me.

"As a civilian, her interference is a hindrance," the other said. "If we let every person who wants to get involved freedom to do whatever they want, chaos will be the result. Vigilantes will rise. She needs to be convinced to stay out of this one especially. Lowery should know better, having been an officer. From the files Davis gave us, these women have been extremely lucky."

Luck and a bit of skill. I smirked.

At the sound of approaching footsteps, I rushed back to the bench and pretended to sleep against Ann's shoulder. I kept my eyes open slightly, hoping whoever came couldn't see through the darkness.

Agent Gavin stared into the cell for several minutes before leaving. I heard the far-off slam of a door and couldn't help but wonder who stayed behind to watch over us. I hoped it was Milton. At least it would be someone I knew.

When I woke again, the pale light of morning streamed through the small window high on the wall. I glanced at the door expecting Eric to be there to take me home. He wasn't.

"It's early," Ann said, patting my arm. "He'll come for us."

I nodded. I knew he would. "How are we going to continue without being arrested again?"

"Carefully." She smiled. "I'm working on it."

I quietly told her what I'd overheard the night before.

"We shouldn't talk here."

Milton arrived with breakfast, which consisted of weak coffee and runny eggs. "Sorry. Sometimes, we have volunteers who cook for the prisoners. Not all of them are good cooks."

"Has Eric or Larry called?"

"They'll be here today. Be patient." He left, his heels clicking against the tiled floor.

Davis was the next to arrive. "Cooking up more trouble during the night, CJ?"

"I don't know what you mean." I sporked a mouthful of eggs into my mouth.

"Agent Gavin said you weren't sleeping when he checked on you ladies."

"He was mistaken. I was exhausted after a full day."

"Uh huh. They won't be as nice if they have to arrest you again."

"Understood." I focused on my food.

"I'm sure Amber is disappointed," Mags said, "to know that her husband has arrested her grandmother for doing nothing more than asking questions."

"Asking questions?" He frowned. "You went to a known gang neighborhood, asked questions, stomped around a crime scene, and had Ann's car vandalized and towed."

I raised my hand. "In our defense, there was no crime-scene tape."

"God spare me." He glanced down the hall. "Thank the Lord above, you ladies are making bail."

"Will we have to go to court?" Mags asked.

"Most likely," he said. "I'm sure it'll be nothing more than a fine. Unless you get arrested again."

Eric approached the cell. "Ready to go home, ladies?"

"Where's Larry?" Mags rushed to the bars.

"Said he had a job to do for you."

"Oh, right." She sniffed and glared at Davis. "I'll be talking to Amber about this."

"I'm sure you will." He unlocked the door and moved back. "See you Sunday for brunch." He turned and headed to his office.

I stepped into Eric's arms. "I have so much to tell you."

He laughed. "I'm sure you do." He gave me a quick hug and kiss, then took my hand and sprang us from jail.

On the way to Grams's house, I filled him in on what we'd done the day before with Ann and Mags interjecting the occasional comment. "We're getting somewhere; we really are."

He nodded. "Larry is getting those maps you want. Once he has them, I'll see if I can't find a way of sneaking up the mountain to see what I can find."

"Not alone. Take someone with you, please."

"I promise I won't be going alone." When he didn't offer who would accompany him, I wanted to demand he tell me, then decided it might be better not knowing. One thing I did know was he wouldn't ask me. He wanted me out of danger as much as I wanted him out as well. The problem was I made his job a lot harder than he made mine.

"It looks as if we're totally disregarding orders from the FBI," Ann said from the backseat.

"Absolutely." I grinned.

Chapter Thirteen

Caper and even Sherlock were ecstatic to see me after my night away from them. Both were on the bed and in my face as I tried to catch up on my sleep.

By mid-afternoon, Larry yelled from the front room for us all to join him at the kitchen table. I groaned, moved my fur babies aside, and tossed off my sheet. Since I'd slept in shorts and a tank top, I padded barefoot to meet up with the others.

"Here you go." Mags handed me a cup of coffee and reached over to pat my hair into place. "Don't you care at all what you look like in front of Eric?"

"She's always beautiful to me." Eric kissed the back of my neck, sending warmth into my face and tingles down my spine.

"I'll go comb my hair." I grinned and took my coffee with me. So much for being lazy. Since I was back in my room anyway, I pulled on a pair of cotton capris, brushed my hair, then pulled my curls into a ponytail. Better. I'd showered before falling into bed, so at least I didn't have the others waiting on me for too long.

When I returned, Larry had spread out a blueprint on the table. "Is that the mountain?"

"Yep. I'm not seeing anything under the ground, but I'm still going with the idea there are mines and tunnels up there somewhere," he said.

"Why?"

He glanced at me, surprise flickering in his eyes. "It's the only thing I can think of as to why this mountain is so important to those crooks for so long."

I shrugged and sipped my coffee. "It's a lot of space to cover on a whim."

"I'll do some each day as part of my job," Eric said. "If there's something up there, I'll find it."

"You promised not to go alone," I reminded him.

"I'll have someone with me as much as I can. I can't stop doing my job, CJ."

"We're dealing with very bad people." My coffee suddenly tasted bitter, and I moved to the sink. After setting it inside, I placed my hands flat on the counter and hung my head.

Eric joined me and turned me to face him. "I will be asking for other rangers to join me, but they can't every day. I'll be careful, and I'll have a weapon."

"Having a weapon won't stop a sniper." I leaned my forehead against his chest.

He tilted my face to his. "Think of it this way. The sooner we find whatever is up there, the sooner we can end all this and stop this crime spree. We're going on a year of one thing after another. Don't you want it to stop?"

"Yes." I'd be doing some searching of my own. I'd buy a side-by-side with some of my inheritance.

The more of us looking, the sooner we'd find...whatever. "I'd like to pay another visit to the prison but speak with Carla Jacobson this time."

"I doubt she'll tell you anything."

"Maybe she can't resist bragging." My phone buzzed, showing a text from Roy asking if I planned on coming into work soon because potential renters have been coming by. I responded I'd be in within the hour. "Work calls. How about supper by the lake tonight?"

"Great idea." He kissed me and went back to study the map.

I spent a few minutes looking it over, snapped a few photos of it, then went to gather my purse and Caper's leash. With purse in hand and leash clipped to my dog's collar, I followed Ann out the door.

"I'd forgotten we have to drive your car. The engine sounds so wimpy."

I rolled my eyes. "I like my car. Stop being a snob. It's good for the environment." Especially now that I needed to drive somewhere.

"Are you really wanting to visit Carla?" Ann asked as we headed toward Heavenly Acres.

"Yes. Will there be a problem?"

"If Davis or the FBI press charges, there will be. We'd best try to go tomorrow. If they proceed with our arrest and the papers get filed, we won't be allowed to visit anyone."

"Gee, if I'd known that, I would have obeyed Davis without question." I grinned.

Ann laughed. "We'll go first thing in the morning."

A car I didn't recognize sat outside my house. A

middle-aged couple waited at my picnic table. A quick glance at the house didn't reveal anything to worry about.

"Good afternoon," I approached them and held out my hand. "I'm CJ Turley, the manager here."

"Joe and Mary Wilson." He returned my shake. "We're interested in looking at one of these tiny houses. If we like it, we'll want to rent every spring and summer, becoming snowbirds of sorts. It's better than the upkeep on a full-sized house for only a few months of the year."

"I have just the place." I led them to the golf cart and drove to house number eleven, a 350-square-foot house with black trim. "This is one of our largest." Other than the ones Roy and his family and the one the Flower family lived in. I glanced in the direction of number six. After only a few days, the Flower house looked forlorn. "Or would you prefer something smaller?"

"Smaller?" Mrs. Wilson scrunched up her nose. "This is barely bigger than our garage."

"The best thing about this one," I said, choosing to ignore her complaint, "is that the bedroom is downstairs. There is a loft for storage, but all living space is downstairs."

"I do like that," the woman said.

Ann waited outside while I let them enter the house. I hovered in the doorway as they examined every little cranny of the shabby-chic interior. "Since the house is fully furnished, it would be perfect for snowbirds."

"How would we know it will be available each spring?" Mr. Wilson asked.

"I'll make sure of it." I smiled. We didn't have many renters during the winter, so it wouldn't be difficult. "With a deposit, you'd be guaranteed."

"It is beautiful here." A smile graced the woman's face. "Joe is quite the fisherman. I paint landscapes and can't wait to put that view in oil." She stared at the lake.

"The chapel might be to your liking, also. It's quaint. Shall I write up the lease?"

Joe nodded. "We'd like to bring our few belongings over in the morning."

As I headed back to my house to get a lease, another vehicle pulled up, this one carrying a family of three. The teenage boy glared sullenly out the window, clearly not impressed.

"Do you think interest is increasing because of the news?" I asked Ann.

"Could be. Maybe Larry posted an advertisement to get business going again. I'm going to want to see the new leases in order to do background checks on these people. I don't trust they aren't being sent by Jose."

"Agreed."

By the time the others arrived for supper, Larry carrying a large crockpot full of potato soup, I'd written three new leases. He nodded when I asked if he'd posted an ad.

"I took a photo of the lake and used it to entice people." He grinned and set the pot in the center of the table. "The lake and the mountain in the background is one of the most beautiful views I've ever seen. Other folks will realize it too, once they've laid eyes on the place."

"I've brought homemade bread," Mrs. Acres sang as she joined us. "Are group suppers a regular thing for y'all?"

"Yes, ma'am." Larry smiled and took the bread. "At the rate we keep growing, we'll need more chairs."

"I've got two folding chairs in the house." I rushed inside, grabbed the chairs from where they hung on the wall, then paused and studied the laughing group around my table outside. Eric was right. This place deserved to be safe and peaceful. That wouldn't happen without us actively putting an end to the danger. I could only pray no one got killed.

"I'm thinking about writing a book," Larry's grandmother said. "About all the crime going on around here. Of course, I'll wait until it's ended, then write a fiction story based on true events." She looked rather proud of herself. "I've already got the first few chapters written. Spent my free time searching the Internet." Her gaze settled on me. "You aren't hard to find out about, Missy. Your name is everywhere."

The chair I was unfolding and I froze. "What do you mean?"

"Clarice Josephine Turley, only remaining family member. I found your phone number, both addresses, and every news article you've been in. Keep it up, and you'll become this town's local celebrity."

I glanced at Ann wondering if my arrest had been spread around yet. She shrugged, reading my mind. No help for it. What was out there was out there. Although it did make it harder to go incognito.

"I've been thinking about your idea of a gated community, CJ," Larry said, dunking a slice of bread into his bowl of soup. "That would be quite the endeavor. We'd have to have two gates. One at the entrance and one where the path to the chapel and campgrounds start. That would mean your view of the lake would be ruined with iron bars."

"Oh. I hadn't thought far enough ahead. It's the best thing I could think of to make this community safer."

"I could head up a neighborhood watch," Mrs. Acres said. "I used to be in one. It isn't difficult."

"We could install a few more cameras," Larry added. "I like the idea of getting the community involved. Make it mandatory that every house takes a one-night rotation."

"You don't think that would discourage renters?" My brows raised. "Perhaps keep it to homeowners rather than renters."

"I'm willing," Mags said. "I've got my Taser, and as Eric can testify, I'm not afraid to use it."

"It's strictly keeping a watchful eye, sweetheart." Larry patted her hand. "No need to engage if you see something suspicious."

"Unless it's one of those kids," his grandmother said. "I've broken up several make-out sessions."

We stared at her.

"What?" Her eyes widened.

"That's not the type of thing we're looking out for," I said.

"Well, there's a curfew here. Those kids are often out past midnight."

"Okay then, yes. Send them home." Poor Danny

and Rose. They must feel like the characters in a young adult romance novel. Now to keep it from becoming tragic.

"Is Danny still doing odd jobs around the community?" Mags asked. "Tire him out so he's too exhausted to get into trouble. Remember…he was a thief at one time."

As if I could forget. One of the first things I'd had to deal with as manager of Heavenly Acres was to find out who was stealing things, one of them being my laptop. "He's changed. Other than hanging with Rose after hours, he doesn't do anything wrong. And, yes, he helps his father after school. In the summers, he still mows the grounds. Danny Olson is not the one we need to be concerned about."

"Then who is?" Mrs. Acres crossed her arms.

"That's what we're trying to find out." I stared at Ann. "It's going to be hard taking our turn when Mags and I are not staying here. Since, as Mrs. Acres kindly pointed out, my information is so easily found, I'm moving home in the morning."

"Me, too." Mags narrowed her eyes at Larry. "Feel free to stay with me if you think I need protection."

"Oh, I will." A muscle ticked in his jaw. My poor uncle knew when he'd lost the battle.

Eric didn't look pleased either. "There isn't room in your house for both Ann and me, but I can pull my house alongside yours, CJ. That way, at least I'll be close."

"Great." I clapped my hands. "We've got a plan. Let's scour a mountain and catch the bad guys." Right after I went face-to-face with a crime lord.

Chapter Fourteen

Either the prison didn't know about our arrest or luck was on our side because Ann and I sat across a table from Carla Jacobson the next morning.

The woman must have agreed to meet us out of boredom, curiosity, or both because the look on her face was anything but friendly. Wary, even. "What do you want?" Her lip curled. "Come to check up on your friend? She's fine other than a black eye. She's clumsy." Carla laughed as if she'd said the funniest joke.

"She isn't our friend," I said. "She tried to kill me once."

"Only once?" Carla tilted her head. "The woman is slacking off." She leaned her elbows on the table, moving her gaze from me to Ann and back to me. "You aren't here for frivolous conversation."

"Let's move this outside." Ann showed her the pack of cigarettes.

"Fine." Carla sauntered out ahead of us.

I glanced over my shoulder on the way out to see

the guard watching. He seemed more intent on us than he had been when we'd visited Addie. I met his sharp stare with one of my own, then joined the other two at one of the picnic tables.

"I've got…contacts," Ann said, sliding the cigarettes across the table. "For your cooperation, I can get your time here reduced."

Suspicion crossed Carla's face. "You want me to snitch? Haven't you heard? Snitches get stitches. Especially in my line of work."

"Which is?" I asked.

"Import, export." She laughed again, then moved to the electric lighter mounted on the fence.

"I don't think she's going to talk," I whispered when the woman stepped away.

"Not in words. Watch body language and listen for what she doesn't say."

Maybe I needed to study how to do that because what Ann said didn't make a lot of sense to me. "I'll let you take the lead."

"Finally." A slight smile cracked Ann's cop face.

When Carla returned, Ann slipped a hundred-dollar bill to her. "This will get me in trouble, but we were already arrested. Just made bail yesterday. I'm sure this will make life a little easier."

"Arrested for what?" Carla pocketed the bill.

"Interfering in a police investigation," I said, grinning. "I'm not so popular down at the station."

"Why are you telling me this?" She blew a puff of smoke in my face.

Doing my best not to cough, I said, "I want to know what's so special about the mountain."

"Have you read any history books lately?" Carla

grinned and took another puff. "There's all kinds of surprises up there, waiting for anyone with ambition to take advantage of. Hiking, horseback riding—"

"We're more interested in illegal activities." Ann breathed sharply from her nose.

"Why would I know anything about that?" Carla's gaze flicked toward the door.

I glanced over to see the guard standing there, arms crossed, a hard glint in his eyes. "A friend of yours?"

"Girl, we make friends in here with anyone we can. It's how we stay alive."

"He doesn't look like your friend."

Carla swallowed hard. "Don't worry about my business."

Now I knew what Ann meant about unspoken words. Carla was scared. Why? She and her husband ran a large, ruthless crime ring. Was Jose a competitor or a partner? Instinct told me I'd hit the proverbial nail on the head. Which meant our stony-faced guard worked for Jose.

I lowered my voice. "Tell me about Jose."

Ann shot me a curious glance. She obviously decided to roll with it because she kept her mouth shut and didn't kick me under the table for taking the lead away from her.

Carla froze. "How did you find out about him?"

"A little birdie."

"He's come up from Mexico to take over our turf. Thinks because Dante and I are locked up, that leaves it wide open for him to swoop in." She laughed without humor. "He's still fishing. The hombre ain't got a clue what treasure the mountain holds."

"Not yet," I said. "But he's got men looking. Who did the fake grounds crew at Heavenly Acres work for?"

Her gaze again flicked to the guard. "Jose."

"Then, he's going to want retaliation, isn't he? That money Ann slipped you might buy you some protection."

"I'm done talking about Jose." She shook another cigarette from the pack. "You want to get me killed?" She headed back to light her cigarette.

The guard joined her.

Carla said something that caused him to glare at us.

He gave a nod and approached the table. "Carla wants you to leave."

"Why?" I asked.

"It don't matter. You ain't her lawyer so she don't have to talk to you."

"What about the cigarettes?" I had no idea why I asked that question, but if this man frightened Carla, he scared me more.

He grinned. "I'll take them." With a glance toward the building, he slipped the pack into his pocket. "Goodbye, ladies."

I groaned and shook my head at Carla as the guard escorted us inside. She followed a few paces back. At the guard's desk, we were handed our IDs and went our separate ways.

"We need to get protection for the Jacobsons," Ann said the minute we got into the car.

"The guard works for Jose. Jacobson killed the three fake grounds-crew men because they were looking for the drugs. Now we're asking Carla questions. Jose wants to take over and...who buried the drugs in the playground?" I tapped my finger against my lip. "It had to be Jacobson's people. The grounds crew was there to find them for Jose." I turned to face Ann. "That meant those drugs were there before the playground was put in, probably before the community was even built. Before Larry purchased the land. Heavenly Acres is in the middle of a gang war."

"Which is why crime happens so often." Ann slapped the steering wheel. "I should have put the pieces together before this."

"How could you? We didn't even know about Jacobson and Jose. Who are we in more danger from?"

"Carla and Dante." She grinned. "If my hunch is right, Jose will use your nosiness to his advantage."

I returned her smile. "Maybe I need to offer him my services."

"Maybe you do. Mags is going to have a fit because she isn't along with us today."

"I'll find a way to pacify her." Besides, she was digging with Larry at the library. We couldn't be together all the time or nothing would get done.

We found Jose exactly where we'd spoken to him before.

"Ladies." He grinned and motioned for us to sit. "You've been busy. My man said you visited Carla this morning."

"News travels fast." I leaned my arms on the table. "What do you want from me?"

He blinked a few times. "Why on God's green earth would I want anything from you?"

"I'm still breathing, aren't I? No one has attempted to kill me."

"Keep asking questions and that will change."

"Is that a threat?"

"It won't come from me, girlie."

I smirked, not believing him. "Here's what I think." I leaned closer. "I think you're watching to see what me and my friends will dig up so you won't have to work as hard. I'm not going to work for you for free."

He laughed, attracting the attention of several others in the bar. "You are a funny little thing. What do you want?"

"My boyfriend is a park ranger. He's going to be riding the trails of that mountain. I want you to make sure nothing happens to him. You do that, and I'll let you know what I find out."

Ann nudged me with her leg.

I returned the gesture. I knew what I was doing. All I could do from this point on was pray it would work. "I also need protection for my friends and myself."

Snapping his fingers, Jose ushered over the same waitress from before. "Call Willie and Daniel. Tell them I need to see them now. Oh, and bring us some chips and salsa and something to drink. My friends need refreshment. Tell Pat to make sure and use his best tequila."

The young woman nodded and hurried away. A few minutes later, she returned with the chips, salsa, tea, soda, and margaritas.

Jose laughed. "I should have specified what you wanted to drink. My people aim to please me."

"Because you'll harm them if they don't," I said, refusing to think him anything but the ruthless thug he was.

He laughed again. "I'm going to enjoy having you around. Your friend here—well, she needs to lighten up."

"Not when my friend is in possible danger."

"Serious bodyguard." He took one of the margaritas. "Here's what I need you to do, ladies. One, I need to know if there are more bags of white powder buried in Heavenly Acres or the campground. Two, I need to know what is so special about that mountain."

"I'm surprised that with the manpower you have, you couldn't find that out." I dipped a chip in the salsa, took a bite, and lunged for the water. Spicy.

"I'm new here. I'm growing my business. That takes time. Anything else I can help you with?"

"Yes. I need a side-by-side, brand new, red and fast, seats four, delivered this afternoon. I'm sure a man of your importance can manage that." I smiled.

A hardness came across his features, but his smile didn't waver. "I'll get you that, little girl, but the safety of your man was what we agreed on."

"True, but I need one and you can get it faster."

"Hmm. Anything else?"

I glanced at Ann who shook her head, then back to Jose. "That'll do it." I stood and offered my hand. "I wouldn't call you a gentleman by any means, but around here we shake on things."

He returned my shake. "Don't disappoint me, little girl."

Outside, Ann whirled. "Are you insane? You

can't tell him anything about what we find. Davis will have you locked up for life."

"I lied. I'll feed Jose just enough to keep him satisfied and Eric safe."

"Lies will get you killed."

"Not unless he finds out. I guess we need to tell Davis what we're doing?" The two FBI agents were going to explode. Somehow, we needed to convince them that we could actually help rather than hinder the investigation. "How do you feel about Mexican food for supper?"

"Sounds good. Since you're such good friends with Jose, maybe we can get the food for free." Ann laughed. "You're a bad influence on me."

We crossed the street and placed an order for enough food for our little group, saying we worked for Jose.

"You work for Jose?" The hostess's eyes widened. "Are you for real?"

I shrugged. "You could go ask him, but that might make him think you're calling him a liar. He won't like that." When had I become so ruthless? Mags would blame it on my night in jail, no doubt. In reality, I just wanted my life back and would do what I needed in order for that to happen.

"Fine. Please have a seat while the cook prepares the food." Back straight, she disappeared into the kitchen.

"I don't think she likes me," I said.

"These people are running scared. They aren't sure who will harm them if they say the wrong thing." Ann shook her head. "It's not a life I'd want to live."

Me either. "We've tossed a lot of rocks into the air. Time to see where they fall."

"And who gets hit on the head."

"That, too." *Please, God, keep me from having made a fatal mistake in aligning with Jose.*

The waitress brought our bags of food. "I called Jose. He confirmed your story and said not to take advantage of your partnership." She handed us the bags.

"Tell him, thank you." I didn't promise not to take advantage. Bad guys didn't deserve any breaks.

Ann and I headed to my car, where thankfully, all four tires remained aired. A sheet of paper waved from under the windshield wiper. I leaned close and read, "If Carla dies, you die."

Chapter Fifteen

I tore the threat from the window, wadded it up, and tossed it in the backseat. I didn't have time for such things. Getting my life back was more important. "Should we tell Davis what we're up to?"

Ann thought for a minute. "He'll find out soon enough on his own. Let's see what we can accomplish before getting arrested again."

True. The minute he knew what we were doing, he'd lock us up for sure. "Let's go feed our troops."

"You did what?" Eric plopped onto the picnic-table bench, almost missing the seat, and windmilled his arms to keep from falling. Once he regained his balance, he asked the question again.

"I've hired you protection." I left out who would be doing the protection. "I've got Ann and figured you needed someone." I forced a big grin.

He crossed his arms. "Who?"

"Oh, you won't see them." I handed him a plate. "We wouldn't want the bad guys to know you're on to them, right?" I hoped I was making sense.

"We're having a talk after supper."

"Uh-oh," Mags whispered, nudging me with her elbow. "I'd like to have a chat too, to find out what you two were really up to."

"Later." I glanced at Eric to see whether he'd heard her. Since he was digging into a chimichanga as if he hadn't eaten in a week, I didn't think so. Larry had heard, though, judging by his narrow-eyed stare in my direction.

What the heck. I didn't want to have to repeat myself. "Jose's goons will be watching over you and us in exchange for my finding out whether the Jacobsons hid any more drugs around here." There.

Everyone but Ann froze and stared as I continued. "In exchange for Jose purchasing me a new side-by-side, I'll be finding out what is so special about this mountain."

"It's been called a lot of things," Larry said, "but it actually has no name. Mags and I have had to dig through the archives just to find out that tidbit. How do you expect to find out anything?"

"That's what you're worried about?" Eric scowled. "Not the fact that these two thick-headed women have aligned themselves with a crime boss?"

All heads turned from me to him. "I'm perfectly safe, Eric," I said. "As long as Jose thinks I'm a benefit to him, he won't hurt me."

"What about Jacobson?"

"Oh. Considering Carla admitted that it was her people who killed the grounds crew who worked for Jose, yeah, that might be something to consider." I grimaced. "We're valuable players in a war, folks. Heavenly Acres is smack dab in the middle of a battlefield."

"Once again, you and Ann have all the fun." Mags cut into an enchilada.

"We had fun," Larry said.

She shook her head. "Going cross-eyed from looking at a computer all day does not classify as fun." She glanced up. "Don't look now, but your grandmother is coming."

"Darn. She'll be mad. I knocked on her door to invite her for supper, but she didn't answer." He stood and went to meet her, taking the plate she carried out of her hands and setting it on the table.

"I brought my own," she said, "although Mexican sounds much better than pot roast."

"There's plenty," I offered.

"Maybe some rice." She squeezed on the other side of Mags. "I thought y'all might want to know there was a black man snooping around the woods last night."

"What?" Larry frowned. "When?"

"About midnight. That's when I decided to do my neighborhood watch." She smiled, clearly pleased with herself. "That's why I had to take a nap. Anyway, I stood in the shadows of my porch and watched a flashlight bob in and out of the trees. At one point, the beam illuminated his face."

"Would you recognize him again?"

"Most definitely, but I won't step foot in the police station. Can't abide the place."

"I'll call Davis," Ann said. "Mum on everything else." She called him and asked that he bring photos of known members of Jacobson's and Jose's gangs for a witness to look over. "Because we're eating supper and she doesn't want to come. She's old."

Ann smiled and hung up. "He isn't happy about coming to us, but he said he'll be here within the hour."

"Good. We can finish eating before he starts yelling and ruins our appetites." Mags resumed eating.

"I don't understand you people, even after almost a year." Eric exhaled heavily. "You lay on me what you've been up to, then eat as if nothing has happened."

I motioned my head toward Mrs. Acres, then shook my head.

"I saw that," the old woman said. "Keep your secrets. They'll all come out soon enough."

Hopefully not until I was ready.

Davis pulled up alongside where Eric's house now resided next to mine. He stared at the houses in close proximity to each other, then shook his head and joined us at the table, dropping some books in front of us. "Who's the witness?"

"I am. Don't be surly." Mrs. Acres started riffling through the pages.

"Is anyone going to fill me in on the suspicious character?" He asked.

"I will when I'm finished here," Mrs. Acres replied.

I gave Davis a sympathetic glance. We'd all been on this side of Mrs. Acres' sharp tongue.

"Fine. CJ, Ann, a minute please. Over there." He headed to the edge of the lake and waited.

"Good luck." Eric gave my hand a squeeze.

I groaned and stood. "I guess he found out about our visit to the prison."

"Looks that way." Ann's lips were pursed as if she'd eaten something sour.

Feeling much like a woman headed to her execution, I squared my shoulders and joined Davis at the water's edge. "Yes?"

"Do you want a criminal record? Are you trying to stay on the FBI agents' bad side?" He leaned closer until our noses almost touched. "Do you want to die?"

"No to all the above."

"Why visit Carla Jacobson in prison?"

"We had some questions. I wanted to know who the three dead guys worked for."

"I gather she told you because now she's dead." He straightened and glared at us.

"It's time to tell you I got a threat today." I grimaced. "A note on my car said if Carla dies, I die."

Davis muttered something unflattering under his breath. "Where were you when you received this threat?"

"In town."

"You're withholding information, aren't you?"

"If I am, it's only because I'm concerned about your blood pressure." I grinned, despite the ice running through my veins.

"What the heck?" He glared over my shoulder as Caper started barking.

I turned to see a truck and trailer pull up. On the trailer was a lovely side-by-side. Two men rolled it off the trailer, tossed Eric the keys, and sped away. "I wasn't expecting it until tomorrow. Awesome."

"Those men look familiar. Who are they?"

"Delivery guys." I shrugged. "Who cares? I got

my new toy."

"Why would a woman whose job is to patrol a relatively small area need one?"

"Stop asking so many questions. Isn't it plausible I want one for recreation? Isn't that what a lot of people use them for?" I crossed my arms and tilted my head. "Questions often get answers you don't want to hear. I promise to tell you everything as soon as I can."

"You've been awfully quiet, Lowery." He turned to Ann. "Anything you want to tell me?"

"I'll keep a close watch on CJ."

He rolled his eyes. "That's a good idea considering the two of you are still interfering with the investigation, and she's received a death threat." His voice rose. "Don't come crying to me if you get killed." He grabbed the books from the table after Mrs. Acres pointed to a page. He stormed to his car and squealed tires on his way out.

"Reckless driving," Mags said. "Wait until I tell Amber."

"Leave him be," Ann said. "CJ's giving him a headache."

"Is that normal?" Mrs. Acres raised a brow. "Because she seems the annoying type."

"I'm right here." Davis would definitely label me as annoying and troublesome. Where would the murder attempt happen? In the woods? On the mountain? In town? There were a lot of possibilities for someone to do away with me. Speed in solving this case became imperativeThe man might shoot me himself with all the demands I made.

"I should have asked Davis if Addie Morris is

alright."

"He would have said if she wasn't, although now that her boss is dead, the target on her back has become bigger. Jose's gang will target everyone associated with Jacobson."

"Did you find the man you saw last night?" I glanced at Larry's grandmother.

"Sure did. Shante Leroy."

Ann typed into her phone. "Rap sheet a mile long. Nothing violent, just petty theft. Works for Jacobson." She glanced up and met my gaze.

I grinned. "If he's here looking around, that means there is still something hidden." I glanced through the dimming light of evening toward the shadows of the woods behind Heavenly Acres. If the man searched the woods, there must not be anything left on the actual community property. Tomorrow, I'd borrow a shovel from Roy and start digging.

Caper stood and put her paws on my leg. Yep, I'd start digging right along with my furry friend.

"You're up to something," Eric said.

"Just going to do some digging. Nothing too dangerous."

"Right." He stood and cleared away the empty food containers. "I'll be heading up the south side of the mountain tomorrow."

"Mags and I will return to the library," Larry said.

"Oh, goody." Mags frowned. "It beats shoveling, though."

"I'll be watching CJ's back," Ann added. "Now, can we go inside where a sniper can't pick us off?"

That lit a fire under us. We scampered to our

houses, Eric joining Ann and me. I dropped the garbage in the nearest trash bin and collapsed onto the sofa.

"It's been a productive day." I nodded, pleased with myself.

"I'd like to go a year or two without someone threatening to kill you." Eric sat next to me, his arm along the back of the sofa. "Do you realize that has never happened during our relationship?"

"That's true. The day I took the job, Ms. Rice told me of the burglaries and suggested I enlist your help." I cupped his face. "You lucky man."

He laughed and kissed the palm of my hand. "I'm the luckiest man in Arkansas."

"Before the two of you get too gushy and make me gag, why would a mountain not have a name?" Ann lowered herself in a chair across from us and petted Sherlock who decided to make her lap his bed.

"Couldn't agree on a name, I guess." Eric shrugged. "The historical society might know."

I face-palmed myself. "Why haven't any of us thought of that before now?" Of course that group of people would know everything historical about this area. I fished my phone from my pocket and texted Larry to add a visit to the society to his task list tomorrow.

We watched a few sitcoms, then Eric excused himself for bed. "I've a full day tomorrow." He leaned over and kissed me. "Try to stay here tomorrow. Give my mind a break."

"I promise to do nothing more than dig for drugs." And find out a little more about Shante Leroy.

Chapter Sixteen

"**All right, girl. Let's** play." Not that I really thought Caper needed the encouragement, but I pretended to dig with my hands at the base of a tree. Within seconds Caper's tail was wagging and she sent dirt flying.

"This is a waste of time," Ann said, leaning on her shovel. "We'd do better questioning the people who work for Jose."

"This is safer. If we find him something, his peeps will be more willing to talk to us. Remember? The waitress was unfriendly to say the least."

"A ride up the mountain?" She raised her brows. "Don't you want to try out your new ride?"

"Later." I wanted to drive the side-by-side very much, but Shante Leroy had been looking for something, and I intended to find out what. Ann could grumble all she wanted. We weren't leaving until I had something. "Start digging."

"I can't watch your back and dig, too."

"You wouldn't be able to stop a bullet." I jammed

the blade into the dirt and scooped.

Caper moved to another plot of ground, nose to the dirt. She gave a bark and started digging.

I decided to let her show me where to dig. My small stature wouldn't allow a lot of useless digging.

"Call her off!" Ann reached down.

"Caper, come here." I snapped my fingers.

Ann held up a bag of white powder and another of marijuana. "Bingo."

"We really need more drug-sniffing dogs out here."

"My thoughts exactly." She sent a text to Davis. "Hide the cocaine. We'll give him the marijuana. That should entice him to start searching again and leave us something for Jose."

I glanced around for a hiding place. The only thing I could think of was one of the houses furthest away from the playground so the dogs wouldn't sniff out what we wanted hidden. Feeling like a criminal, I darted across the playground and into house number twenty-two. I stashed the drugs in the freezer before returning to Ann. "Dogs can't smell through the door of a freezer, can they?"

"No idea. Let's head back to your house to wait for Davis. I don't like how easily someone can sneak up on us out here. We can do some research on Leroy."

"Sounds good. I could use another cup of coffee." I leaned the shovel against the side of Roy's house, Ann doing the same, then called for Caper to follow me home. Since she was having so much fun digging, I had to call her a dozen times. By now, Davis and Milton had parked next to my house.

"I meant to ask," Davis said. "Why is Eric's house next to yours?"

"He thinks it's safer. Want some coffee?"

"Yes," both men said in unison.

While the three of them sat at the outside table, I headed in to make three cups of coffee one at a time with my tiny coffeepot. I strained my ears to hear their conversation, but they kept their voices lowered. Were they talking about me? They had to be.

I set four mugs of brew on a tray and rushed outside. Yep. Talking about me because they clamped their mouths shut and gave me forced smiles. "You three are horrible." I set the tray in the middle of the table and glanced around for the missing Milton.

Davis lifted a mug and glared at me over the rim. "Why are you digging?"

"Caper found the pot."

"Then why are there two shovels with fresh dirt leaning against Roy Olson's house?"

Nosy detective. "I was helping my dog. Didn't Ann give you what we found?"

"Yes." He blew into his cup. "Why do I feel as if you're withholding information from me?"

A change of subject was in order. "What I find suspicious is the fact that other than introducing themselves and arresting me, we've not seen FBI agents Gavin and Thompson."

"Their business is not yours." His eyes narrowed. "I will find out what you're up to."

"Don't you have a wedding to plan?"

"You make that difficult for me, CJ. Amber is

getting frustrated with all the time I'm spending at work. I'd like to think about starting a family, but it's next to impossible when I'm not home."

"It isn't my fault Caper found those bags in the first place." I'd apologize to Amber the first opportunity I had.

Milton rejoined us. "Evidence of more than one hole, and some were dug with a shovel as you expected." He tilted his head in my direction.

"You already know I was digging."

"What else did you find, CJ?" Davis asked. "If I find out you're lying, I'll throw the book at you."

"Fine. We found another bag of cocaine. I hid it so we can take it to Jose in exchange for information."

Davis's face darkened to the point I thought he'd have a stroke. "Tell me you're not talking about Jose Riveras."

"I don't know his last name. Big guy, flashy grin, shiny ring."

"Heaven help us." Davis stood and paced. "Carla Jacobson isn't going to be the only fatality. You've gotten yourself in the middle of a gang war."

I nodded. "I'm trying to get us out."

"By making friends with a crime boss."

"Yes."

He drew air slowly through his nose, then exhaled and repeated. He stared heavenward for a few seconds, then sat back down. "If you're going to do this, then we're going to work together. You might be onto something. We've not been able to pin anything on Riveras. You can help us do that."

"Like a double agent?" I grinned.

"Sure. You can call it that." He put a hand over mine in a foreign gesture. I can't ever remember him touching me. "You have to do what I say and let me know every single step you take. This is dangerous, CJ. Tell me what your group of misfits are up to." He straightened and turned back to his coffee.

I told him of Mrs. Acres forming a neighborhood watch and of Larry and Mags doing research at the library. I told him how I wanted to bribe Jose with the cocaine and how in exchange for the drugs he had people watching over Eric. "Now, Ann and I were going to ask some questions about Shante Leroy. I'm sure Jose knows who he is."

"He knows everyone involved in this." Davis cupped both hands around his cup and stared at the liquid inside. "I'll be tracking your every movement. Make sure your phone is on you at all times. I'll put a wire on you if I have to."

"I'll make sure both of our phones are on," Ann said. "Sometimes, Jose insists on talking to CJ alone."

"In your sight, though, right?"

"Yes."

"CJ." His gaze speared me. "This man is not only involved in drugs. He's also into trafficking. You look younger than you are. Do not be alone with him or eat or drink anything you haven't seen prepared."

Oops. Already done that. "Okay." His words sent worry scurrying up and down my spine.

"We're getting close. Try and stay alive until this is over." He finished his coffee and pushed to his feet. "Let me know if you want Milton to stake out tonight."

"That won't be necessary." I smiled at the look of relief that flickered across the other officer's face. "He's needed more helping you."

Ten minutes later, I'd locked my pets in my house, Davis and Milton had left, and Ann and I were headed to see Jose with a bag he couldn't refuse. I prayed we wouldn't get into an accident or pulled over. It would take a whole lot of explaining why we had an illegal substance in my trunk, and we'd find ourselves locked up before they could get ahold of Davis to clear things up.

Ann kept glancing in the rearview mirror. After the fifth time, I started to get nervous. This wasn't her usual paranoia. "Is someone following us?"

"I think so. See that dark green sedan two cars back? It's stayed that distance from us since we left Heavenly Acres."

"Can you lose them?"

"Probably not in your car." She pressed harder on the accelerator.

I tightened my seatbelt and kept an eye on the green vehicle. "You should let me drive so you can shoot out their tires."

"Are you nuts? There are other drivers on this road."

"I know, but eventually it'll be just the two of us. That's always how it works on crime shows."

"Not this time. I'm staying where we're surrounded by other vehicles."

Smart plan. They wouldn't try anything with other cars around. Wrong. "Uh, they're getting closer."

"Yep. My guess is because there's no close exit

for me to take." Ann increased our speed again.

"I thought you wanted to stay surrounded by people."

"I did, but I'm not going to endanger them if I can help it." She whipped the steering wheel left and turned around in one of those cleared spaces in the median that civilians weren't supposed to use. We raced back the way we'd come.

The green car followed.

I wasn't sure I wanted to lead them home. "Where are we going?"

"To the police station, I hope. Call Davis."

I did, telling him the color of the car and the mile marker we just passed. "I can't see how many are in the other car. We're managing to stay just far enough...uh-oh."

"Uh-oh, what?" he asked.

"They're going to ram—" I screamed as my head whipped forward, then rammed against the seat back. "You might want to hurry, Detective." I pressed the button to hang up and gripped the dashboard as the car hit us again.

The second hit set us into a spin. Ann fought the wheel, straightening us out and shot us back the way we'd come, down the wrong side of the Interstate. "Hold on. It's going to be a bumpy ride." She shot across the median.

We bounced through a shallow ditch, up a slight incline, down again, and headed in the right direction, except away from home. "All we have to do is stay ahead of them until help arrives, right?"

"Right. I'll be using whatever driving skills I possess," she said, muttering that it wasn't much.

We veered back and forth across the median to the blaring of horns, obscene gestures thrown out of windows, and the occasional squeak from me. Where were the police? I was going to have a chat with Jose. This was not what I called protection.

The far-off sound of sirens filled me with hope. Finally.

Two squad cars raced past us on the other side of the road, then pulled into a clearing. When the green car passed them, they pulled out behind. Another squad car came from behind a stand of trees. The sedan was surrounded.

"Awesome!" I gave Ann a high-five. "That's the way it's done, girlfriend."

A black truck missing a headlight came from a single-lane road that followed the Interstate. He burst through barbed wire and headed straight for us.

I screamed.

The truck rammed into the passenger side.

Airbags deployed.

My pretty little Prius careened off the Interstate and crashed into a tree.

Chapter Seventeen

I opened my eyes to see two black men staring through the shattered window at me. No, make that one. I blinked my eyes to clear my vision. "Shante Leroy?"

"It wasn't me that ran you off the road." He tugged at the car door. "I'm in that red Ford."

"Put your hands up!" Davis's voice cracked as he yelled the order.

"I didn't do it, man." Shante stepped back.

Groaning, I put a hand to my head and checked on Ann. Her forehead lay pressed against the steering wheel. Blood dripped onto her practical black pants. "Ann?" I gingerly shook her arm.

"Don't touch me."

"Good. You're alive." I unhooked my seatbelt and got on my knees to climb through the no-longer-there windshield.

Milton had Shante off to the side.

Noticing me, Davis rushed over to help me to the ground. "Ambulance is on the way."

"Ann is bleeding pretty bad from a head wound." I collapsed on the grass and glanced around for the truck. Nowhere in sight. I waved at Milton. "I'd like to talk to that man."

He didn't look as if he thought it a good idea, but he led Shante over, and with a firm hand on his shoulder, pushed him to sit next to me. "Don't try anything."

"I told you I ain't here to hurt her." Shante's eyes widened.

"Why are you here?" I asked. "Thank you for trying to get me out of the car."

"Welcome." He shot Milton a glance. "I know what car you drive. I saw the black truck come out of nowhere. I backed off until you…crashed, then parked and came running."

"So, you were following me." I lay on my back and stared up through the branches of a tree. I couldn't help but remember the time I lay in the mud, face down, during a torrential downpour and almost drowned because a branch held me down. Were trees going to be my demise?

"You okay?" He peered into my face.

"Why were you following me?"

"To see where you went and what you found." His eyes widened as Davis removed the bag of cocaine from my trunk.

The detective shot me a furious look, then dropped the stuff into an evidence bag. With a shake of his head, he headed to the squad car as an ambulance pulled to a stop on the road's shoulder.

"I can't believe I missed that. Dante is going to kill me."

That answered my unspoken question about whether the gang leader was still alive. "He's probably real mad about Carla, huh?" I returned to a sitting position.

"Yeah, but you didn't kill her. He knows that. It's Jose he wants." Shante smirked. "He wants you to lure Jose into the open so we can get him."

I wasn't sure I had what it took to be a triple agent. "I'll see what I can do." The knock on my head must have made me insane.

Paramedics loaded Ann onto a stretcher, then into the ambulance before coming to check on me. I guess the sight of me sitting up and talking let them know I wasn't about to die. At least not at the moment.

"So, who was in the black truck?"

Shante shrugged. "No one I know. Must work for Jose."

Jose's men were supposed to protect them. Did we have a couple of rogue gangsters on the loose? That would definitely complicate things. Oh, my head hurt.

I refused a ride on the gurney but did allow the paramedic to put an arm around my waist and lead me to the ambulance. "Come see me, Shante. I have a lot of questions."

"I'll try, Miss, but no guarantees. I got to follow orders."

I nodded and climbed into the ambulance.

"Don't leave the hospital until I get there," Davis jabbed a finger in my direction as the paramedic started to close the doors.

I glanced at the medic inside checking Ann's

pulse. "Can I have something for a headache? I'm going to need it." My eyes closed, and I fell off the stool I sat on.

The next time I woke, I lay on a hospital bed, hooked up to a blood-pressure cuff with Ann in a bed a few feet away. "Doc said you have a concussion," she told me.

"I could've figured that out on my own." I pressed the button to raise my bed to a sitting position.

"Your car is totaled. Now you can get something with some speed."

"Do you really think that's wise if I'm driving?" I grinned past the pain of a pounding head, thankful to be alive to think about a new car. "It'll be a few days before we make a trip up the mountain."

"It'll be at least a week, Miss Turley." A smiling doctor of Asian descent approached my bed. "You'll not be doing anything strenuous for that long, and the first two days do nothing, please."

"I have a job. People count on me."

"You'll have to delegate, same as Miss Lowery." He signed something on a clipboard. "We're getting your release papers ready. Is someone coming to get you two?"

"Someone will be here soon," Ann said. "Davis knows."

I lay back on my pillow glad to be going home but not happy about the restrictions.

I dozed off again and woke to Eric kissing me. "That's the best thing to wake up to. Davis must have called you."

"He did." He smoothed hair away from my face.

"That's quite a goose egg you've got. Are you okay?"

I nodded slowly so I wouldn't jostle my head. "I will be. Help me up." I held out my hand.

Instead, he wrapped his arms around me and gently helped me to my feet. "Woman, you scare me. I've never driven as fast down the mountain as I did today. I thought you had protection."

"So did I." I intended to find out what happened to that so-called protection at the first opportunity. "Is Davis here?"

"No, he said to text him when we get home, and he'll meet us there."

A few minutes later Ann and I were being wheeled from the hospital. Eric drove slower than necessary. When we arrived, Mags and Larry waited at the outside table. Two empty lounge chairs waited for the invalids—Mags's words, not mine.

I lowered myself gingerly into one, enjoying the feel of the sun on my face. "I'd like to see Caper, please." I thanked God for the fact I'd left her at home. I didn't want to think about her little body being hurled through the windshield.

Eric brought not only my pup but a cup of coffee. "You look drowsy."

"Thank you, this will not keep me awake." The effects of a pain pill dulled my senses a bit. I didn't want to go to bed only to be awakened by Davis. "I bet you aren't upset about missing today's adventure." I smiled at Mags.

"Nope." She laughed. "That's one you can keep to yourself." Her eyes twinkled. "Larry and I have had a good day ourselves."

"Sure did." Larry set a hardback book on the table. "I reckon you can't see well from that chair, but this is a book about a plantation on No-Name Mountain. Yep, that's the name. Two warring families couldn't decide since they both owned half."

Comfort no longer mattered. I set Caper down and moved to the bench. Picking up the book, I ran my hand over the smooth picture of a plantation house. "Is the house still there?"

"No, but what is there—somewhere—are tunnels." Larry took the book and flipped through the pages. "Tunnels used to smuggle out slaves." He turned the book where I could see.

"Do you think this is the treasure? Where do the tunnels come out?"

"I don't know, but imagine how easy it would be to get drugs or people from one place to the next without detection." He grinned.

"Which is why the drones never found anything." My grin matched his. "This is a fabulous find."

"Don't even think about going up there for a week," Ann said. "Doctor's orders. Besides, my head couldn't take the bouncing around. Neither could yours."

"I have to agree with Ann." Eric met my gaze. "Give yourself a few days to heal. I promise I'll help you look when you're ready."

"Can I at least go talk to Jose? I need to know why he betrayed me."

Eric's eyes flashed. "Only if I go with you." He took my hand. "Stop trying to protect me and let's protect each other. I don't want to be here without you, CJ."

I didn't want to be without him either. "Okay. No more playing mama bear." At least I'd try.

Davis arrived, his eyes landing on the book, then they darted to Ann who had fallen asleep. He turned to me. "I'm surprised to see you up."

"Not sleepy."

"Your droopy eyes tell a different story." He sat next to Mags. "Shante Leroy told me what he saw of the truck. Now you tell me."

I recounted the entire chase on the Interstate by the dark green car. "We didn't see the truck until right before it rammed us. What about those in the car?"

"In jail."

I widened my eyes. "Are you going to tell us who they are?"

"No." A muscle ticked in his jaw. "I'm going to tell you to back off. You almost got killed today. Eric, make her listen."

"I'm trying."

"Where is Shante?" I asked, hoping he hadn't been arrested.

"Home, I guess. I didn't have anything to charge him on." Davis looked sad at that. "The two who are behind bars refuse to talk about who hired them. Shante says he's never seen them before or that truck."

"Hired hands." Mags slapped the table. "Jacobson or Jose hired men to harm Ann and CJ. When the car failed, they sent in the truck."

"You might be onto something, sweetheart." Larry kissed her cheek.

Davis squared his shoulders. "Now that we have

that out of the way, why don't you tell me about this book? I know you aren't passing it around as light reading."

Larry told him of our theory about the tunnels. "I guarantee if you find those tunnels, you'll find out why folks are fighting over this area."

"I agree." Davis stood. "I'll let the FBI know. They have the manpower for a hunt this size. Follow orders and take it easy, CJ. Please."

I almost told him I intended to visit Jose the next day, but since Eric didn't say anything, I kept my mouth shut, too. "One week," I told the others after Davis drove away. "I'll wait one week before riding up that mountain to find those tunnels." No way was I going to let the FBI have all the fun. If anyone saw them up there, they'd run and hide. I, on the other hand, could draw bad guys out of the woodwork like cockroaches.

Chapter Eighteen

The next morning, I sat across from Jose at his usual table in the bar. The man shoveled eggs into his mouth as if he hadn't eaten in days. From the way he'd scowled when Eric and I entered, I thought it best to wait until he'd finished before demanding answers.

When he pushed his plate away, he held up a hand. "It wasn't me."

Was everyone going to deny trying to kill me? "Then who was it? Jacobson? Because one of his men—"

He shook his head. "Neither. There's a new party in town, and I haven't received an invitation."

"But why try and kill me? I have no idea who they are."

He shrugged. "I heard the cops removed something valuable from your trunk. That means there is still drugs on your land. I'll send some guys over to dig it up."

"Absolutely not. I'm not going to put my tenants

at risk from a war starting on the playground." I crossed my arms.

Jose glanced at Eric. "Is she always this difficult?"

"Yep." Eric grinned. "It's part of her charm."

Pat, the bartender, was wiping down a nearby table and seemed far too interested in our conversation. I motioned my head in his direction to alert Jose.

"Hey, some privacy here." Jose waved a dismissive hand toward the guy. "Pat's been sulky ever since I called in his loan. He ought to be happy I let him stay on as bartender."

"You're a loan shark in addition to everything else?" I wondered whether Davis knew. Of course, he did. He knew most things before I did and wasn't as good at sharing information.

"A man needs multiple avenues of income in today's world, little girl."

The man ought to try something more legal. "You aren't doing a good job of protecting me." I moved my bangs to show him the purple and blue goose egg on my forehead. "I'm suffering from a concussion and I'm on pain pills."

"You could get twenty dollars apiece for those." He winked.

I rolled my eyes. "No thanks." Noticing Pat's attention still focused on us, I said, "That man hates you."

"He's harmless. Tries to look tough."

He succeeded, in my opinion. "Try to do better on your part of the bargain or I won't be around to find anything." I pushed to my feet, shot a glare toward the nosy bartender, then linked my fingers with Eric. "I'm ready to go home now."

Less than a mile down the road, Eric informed me we were being followed. I turned in my seat, my heart in my throat. "Not again." I didn't think I could survive another car crash so soon.

"It's the FBI. Black Suburban. I saw them in it the other day when I went into town."

"They'll know we were visiting Jose."

"Yep." His gaze flicked back and forth between the rearview mirror and the road.

"Will they'll pull us over?"

"We didn't do anything wrong. They're just watching and waiting." He reached over and squeezed my hand. "The feds are just figuring out how good you are at finding clues."

"That's because I'm tenacious."

"Yes, you are." He raised my hand to his lips before releasing it and putting both hands on the steering wheel.

When we arrived home, Eric got me settled into bed for a nap. Ann already snored from the sofa. "I'll take care of lunch and supper."

"Don't you have work?"

"Other than a quick ride around the campground, I'm staying with you today. I'll return to work tomorrow." He gave me a tender kiss and left, locking the front door on his way.

Caper and Sherlock curled up next to me. Seconds later, the three of us slept.

It must have been the meds because I dreamed of bartenders, crime bosses, and little old ladies. At one point, Mrs. Acres hit Jose over the head with a cast-iron skillet, causing me and my friends to laugh and laugh until I woke up.

I blinked against the afternoon sun coming in my window. When I realized I truly was awake and not dreaming, I headed downstairs where Ann sat with her laptop.

"How are you feeling?" I asked, sitting across from her.

"Like someone is hitting me in the head with a rubber mallet. You?"

"The same. What are you doing?"

"Looking up every known associate of Dante Jacobson and Jose Rivera. There's something we're overlooking."

I nodded. "Did you know Jose was also a loan shark? He called in the loan on that bar where he holds court."

Her gaze jerked from the laptop to me. "No, I didn't. I'll contact my contact."

"When am I going to meet him?" I wiggled my brows, stopping abruptly when pain traveled to my knot.

"I don't—" She frowned as Caper tore down the stairs, yapping. Ann picked up her gun from the coffee table and yanked open the front door.

Joe and Mary Wilson from number eleven jumped back with wide eyes.

"Can I help you?" Ann kept the gun behind her.

"Oh, uh," Mary stammered. "We need to sign the lease?"

"You already signed it," I said, struggling to my feet. Surely, they wouldn't have both forgotten to put their signatures it.

"Were you eavesdropping?" Ann demanded.

"Of course not." Bill acted indignant.

"Then why come up here with some idiot excuse?" Ann's cop face slipped into place.

"Fine. We've come to complain about the old woman in number twenty. She stands in her window all hours of the day and night, peering through binoculars. The wife and I don't have any privacy for, well, you know."

I bit back a laugh. "Have you tried closing your curtains?"

"We shouldn't have to during the day," Mary said, her brow creasing. "The woman is a meddlesome pervert. Are you going to talk to her?"

"Yes." I sighed. "I'll do it now. Thank you for telling me your concerns. Your satisfaction is of the utmost importance." It didn't sound like I meant the words, but I did.

I clipped Caper's leash on her since I was in no condition to chase her down if she decided to be naughty, then followed Ann out of the house. Neither of us spoke as we strolled around the community. Any sudden jarring of my foot caused my head to ache more.

I glanced back to see Sherlock sitting in the window of my house, his yellow-eyed gaze following us. Could a cat be trained to a leash? I hated always leaving him behind.

Mrs. Acres came down her steps as we approached. "I didn't expect to see the two of you wandering around."

"We've had a complaint. May we sit?" Without waiting for a reply, I lowered myself into a chair next to her outside table. "Some of the tenants are complaining about your spying on them."

"I do not spy on the tenants." She hiked her chin. "I watch the woods and strangers. You should be glad I do because there was more activity last night."

Ann and I glanced at each other, then back at her.

"Explain," Ann said, sitting next to me.

"Not one, not two, but three men were in the woods last night. Big men, Caucasian, wearing hats pulled low over their faces." Mrs. Acres looked pleased with herself.

"Would you recognize them if you saw them?"

"No, but that young man I saw earlier—the one I pointed out in the book—he was hiding and watching, too. He stood right over there behind the Olson house."

"Are you sure he wasn't with them?" I asked.

"Positive. When they left, he went in the opposite direction. That young man was spying for someone."

Ann drummed her fingers on the table. "What were the three men doing? Did they have shovels?"

"Nope. They stood together, then moved away from each other. It looked like they were counting their steps. Would you like some tea? It's sweet and just brewed."

"I'd love a glass," I said. When she went back into her house, I turned to Ann. "Like they were marking a treasure spot."

"It seems that way, but wouldn't it be Jacobson's men who would do that? Jose's wouldn't know where to start looking. Shante works for Jacobson."

"Oh, I forgot to tell you. Jose said there's a third group in town."

"Are you kidding me?" Ann put her head on folded arms. "This is the most twisted, tangled thing I've ever gotten involved in."

"What's up?" Mags popped out from around the house.

"Don't startle us." I narrowed my eyes. "We're injured and can't be jumping." I filled her in on our news.

"Really?" She clasped her hands together. "This is so exciting."

"How so?" My friend had lost her mind.

"Three warring gangs."

"Which is dangerous."

"No one's been killed except Carla Jacobson."

"Not true, "Ann said, glancing at her phone. "I just got word that Dante hanged himself in prison."

"Murdered, you mean. Why would someone with as much power as he had kill himself?" It didn't make sense.

"I need to make a call." Ann moved a few feet away. I suspected it might be her boyfriend.

Mrs. Acres carried out a tray with a pitcher of tea and three glasses. Seeing Mags, she set the tray on the table and went inside for another glass. "Might as well get some cookies, too," she said. "I didn't realize I'd be having an impromptu get-together."

Ann returned. "My informant said the authorities are saying suicide for now but treating his death as a homicide."

A black suburban drove up and stopped. FBI agents Gavin and Thompson got out and strode toward us. They stared through mirrored sunglasses.

"What are you?" Mrs. Acres asked, returning.

"The men in black here to catch some aliens?"

Ignoring her, they faced me. "We need to ask you some questions about Jose Rivera. Where is Mr. Drake?"

"I think he's at the campground. What's this about?"

"Please step aside, Miss Turley." They led me to the other side of the vehicle.

"We know you and Mr. Drake visited Rivera this morning," Agent Gavin said.

"Yes, so?"

"He's been found dead. Blunt-force trauma. You're one of the last people to have seen him alive."

I gasped. Jose had been killed almost exactly like in my dream.

Chapter Nineteen

"What do you know about his death, Miss Turley?" Agent Thompson crossed his arms. I bet he was glaring behind his sunglasses.

"Nothing really, but I dreamed Jose was hit over the head by a skillet. I blamed it on my pain meds." I couldn't help but glance toward Mrs. Acres.

"A dream or a memory?"

"Of course, it was a dream. Don't be ridiculous. Neither me nor my friends are killers, even of bad guys. At least not if we can help it."

"We know everything you've done in the last year," Agent Gavin said. "I advise you to be careful in the future."

"What did you speak to Rivera about?" Agent Thompson asked. If not for the movement of their lips and the words coming out of their mouths, I'd think the two men were carved from Mount Rushmore.

"I, uh—" I was a horrible liar. "We spoke about, uh…why he's so interested in this mountain." Yeah.

That should work.

"You went to a known crime boss to ask questions?" Gavin arched a brow. "You're either brave or stupid."

"I prefer brave." I forced a smile. "Is that all you need from me? My head is pounding, and I'd really like to go lie down."

"We were surprised to see you up and about so soon," Thompson said.

"I still have a job, gentlemen. Do you always talk in plural?" I cocked my head. "Where was Jose killed?"

"That is classified," Gavin said

"Was it with a skillet?"

"Also classified," Thompson added.

These two were nothing like Davis. There would be no give-and-take with them. Hopefully, we could find out something from Ann's resource. "What about Addie Morris? Are you keeping her under protection?"

"She is not your concern," Gavin said, pivoting toward the Suburban.

Thompson lowered his sunglasses, revealing blue eyes. "People around you tend to die, don't they? Perhaps having you around is beneficial. All the crime bosses seem to be getting themselves murdered." He put the glasses back in place and followed his partner.

What a mean thing to say and completely untrue. Sort of. Dante and Jose were dead. Now to figure out the elusive third party who now had no competition.

I returned to my friends and recounted my conversation with the agents. "Can you find out anything?" I asked Ann.

"On it." She typed on her phone as I recounted my strange dream.

Mrs. Acres folded to the bottom step. "The agents are wrong. You weren't one of the last people to speak with Mr. Rivera. I was."

"What?" I frowned. "Did you kill him?"

"No, but I did ask him to find another place for his silly games." She put a hand to her mouth. "If the police find out, I'll be a suspect. I wore a hair net and gloves, you know, to hide my DNA."

She must have been quite the sight. "Was anyone around when you spoke with him?"

"A bartender and a waitress were outside smoking, so they saw me approach the building. I actually spoke with Jose as he walked to his car." She hung her head. "My grandson is going to be livid."

"As he should be," Ann said. "Going alone was foolish and dangerous."

"Pshaw." She waved a dismissive hand. "I've lived a good long life, but I don't want to die of boredom."

"How did you get to town?" I asked.

"I called an Uber. Great. That's one more person who can testify I was there. Do I need to turn myself in?"

Since the Suburban was heading back in our direction, I didn't think she'd have to. "I have a feeling we've temporarily lost the head of our neighborhood watch."

"I'll take over," Mags said. "I used to be in charge before she came." I sensed jealousy.

"I pass the mantle to you." Mrs. Acres stood and

squared her shoulders.

The agents approached at a brisk clip. "Mind coming with us?" Gavin asked her.

"Do I have a choice?"

"No, ma'am."

She held out her hands. "Then I'll be coming. CJ, call me a lawyer."

"We won't be cuffing you, Mrs. Acres," Thompson said. "Unless we need to."

"They're cold and painful," Mags said. "I'd advise against it."

"Okay. I'll come along peacefully." The older woman strode to the vehicle, head high and back straight, house slippers flopping.

"Aren't you going to read her rights?" Mags called out.

"She isn't under arrest…yet." Gavin opened the back door to the Suburban and helped Mrs. Acres inside.

"Mags, call Larry. I don't know any lawyers." Considering how abrasive his grandmother could be, I felt certain she'd be released on bail in no time. They couldn't possibly think her capable of murder.

"My contact says Jose was found behind the bar by the waitress. An iron bar, covered in his blood, was next to him," Ann said, reading a text.

"Then Mrs. Acres couldn't possibly have done it. She wouldn't have the strength to wield such a thing, right?" I glanced from Ann to Mags. "Could you?"

"I'm twenty years younger." She scowled. "Of course, I could. But Larry's grandmother has spaghetti arms. She probably couldn't wave that skillet you dreamed about."

I thought the woman stronger than she looked but kept my mouth shut. "How long until we know whether she's being arrested?"

"My contact will keep us informed," Ann said. "Ready to head back? I need something for my head."

"Sure, we can take the party to your house," Mags said. "Larry will meet us there once he gets a hold of Eric."

I was pretty sure the FBI agents were headed to the campground before turning around to apprehend Mrs. Acres. I glanced at the tree line before turning toward home. What are you hiding, No Name? Where are your underground tunnels?

The sound of Eric's side-by-side approaching had me wishing I could take mine for a drive. Poor Jose. My steps faltered at the thought the FBI agents might confiscate it if they knew where I got it. Could they do that?

I climbed onto the front seat and ran my hand over the red vinyl seats, then opened the glove compartment. It held a user's manual and a folded sheet of paper.

"What's that?" Ann glanced over my shoulder.

"I'm fixin' to find out." I unfolded the paper and spread it on the seat. "It's a map of the tunnels." Grinning, I glanced up at her. "Jose gave it to us."

"Does it say where the entrance is?"

I shook my head. "Not that I can tell, but look." I traced one of the tunnels with my finger. "It definitely goes through part of the mountain." I'd driven through some tunnels made for cars to pass through, but this was far more exciting. "I don't care about doctor's orders. I'm going up there tomorrow."

"Wait and see what Eric says." She stepped back.

"About what?" He leaned in, smiling.

I showed him the map. "Feel like taking a picnic lunch up No Name tomorrow?"

"Sure, but we'll turn around the instant you're in pain."

"Deal." I held up my hand for him to help me from the vehicle, grabbing the map on my way out. "Did Larry tell you about his grandmother?"

"Yes, he's on his way now to see if he can post bail." He walked next to me back to the house and got me settled at the outside table. "I'll get your pill and something to drink."

"I don't want a pill. I need a clear head, but thank you. A drink would be wonderful." I spread the map on the table. Why would Jose give this to me? "Do you think it was in the glove compartment the whole time?"

"No, I think someone put it there after he was killed," Ann said. "Most likely while we were at Mrs. Acres' house."

"Wouldn't we have seen them?" My eyes widened and my mouth dropped open. "Bill and Mary Wilson. That's what they were doing when you caught sight of them outside the window." I looked over at number thirteen. Somehow, I doubted we'd be seeing the snowbirds again.

When Eric joined us, I told him of my suspicions. "I want to go check out their house. Maybe we'll find a clue to tell us whether I'm right or not."

"Hop in the cart. I'll drive." Eric handed me a glass of diet soda.

I took a quick sip and set it on the table, then made sure Caper was secured to her outdoor line. The poor thing hated being tied up, but I couldn't risk her running off right now. "I won't be gone long, sweetie. Then I'll give you a treat to make up for everything." I patted her head and glanced to where Sherlock still sat in the window, his favorite spot during the afternoon.

"Don't you have to give notice of entering a rented house at least a day before?" Eric asked.

"These are extenuating circumstances," I said, sliding from the cart. "I doubt they're coming back anyway."

I climbed the three steps to the front door and unlocked it. After waiting a few seconds for someone to confront me, I said, "Hello?"

No one answered, so I waved the other two inside. "We're looking for anything to tell us whether they worked for Jose."

"Either they were poor, which I doubt, considering they drove an Audi," Ann said, "or you're right and they didn't plan on staying long."

"Why?"

"Other than what came with the house, everything looks like it came from the dollar store." She held up a cheap plastic cup and looked at the tag on the button. "Yep. Dollar store."

"I'll take the bedroom," I said.

"I'll search the loft." Eric climbed the ladder attached to the wall next to the galley-style kitchen.

The bedroom held the supplied queen-size bed with nothing more covering it than a set of sheets and a plain navy-blue blanket. I always assumed renters wanted to add a personal touch to their bedding. Beside and above, shelves and closets provided storage. Drawers were pulled from under the bed. I decided to start there.

It felt strange rifling through people's undergarments, but again I was surprised at how little the Wilsons had. I didn't find any clues in the closet either. "Y'all finding anything?"

"Nope," Ann called back.

"Nada," Eric said.

I climbed on the bed to reach the upper shelves. A half-full coffee cup sat on the lowest one as if someone had fallen asleep without finishing it. I shook my head and used a nearby sock to pick up the cup. The last thing I wanted was a coffee stain across the sheets.

My eyes fell on the coaster underneath that read Jose's. Bingo. I at least had proof they'd been to the bar. "Who wants to pay a visit to a certain bartender?"

Chapter Twenty

"Now?" Eric asked as I showed him and Ann the coaster.

"Why not now? We can stop by and see what's going on with Mrs. Acres while we're in town." I tilted my head. "We can grab supper, too."

"It's a lot to do while both of you have concussions."

I glanced at Ann. "We won't be doing anything strenuous."

She shrugged. "Sure. Let's go. I was looking forward to some TV, though."

Me, too, since my favorite crime drama was on. "It'll be recorded."

At my house, I fed the animals and grabbed my purse, dropping the cardboard coaster inside. Caper promptly ate and fell asleep on the sofa. Sherlock stayed on his favorite perch on the windowsill. He swiped at me when I tried to lower the blinds. "Fine, you little brat." I ruffled the hair on top of his head. "Have it your way." I lowered the blinds halfway, popped a couple of ibuprofen, pocketed the bottle, and then joined the others at Eric's jeep. I tossed the bottle to Ann and climbed into the front seat.

"Thanks." She shook a couple of tablets into her hand and settled into the back with Mags. "This ought to help get me through the next few hours. Where to first?"

"How about jail, supper, bar?" Eric suggested. "I'd rather talk to the bartender when there's a lot of people around."

"Sounds good to me." I clicked my seatbelt into place.

Larry sat in the reception area of the police department, a scowl on his face. "They haven't let me talk to her yet or told me anything."

"Where's Davis?" I asked.

"Haven't seen him either. I don't like this. My grandmother shouldn't be in jail. She isn't a killer." He clasped his hands together tight enough to turn his knuckles white.

"I'll text Davis." Eric pulled his phone from his pocket. Minutes later, he told us Davis was in the room with Mrs. Acres and the agents and would be out as soon as the cantankerous woman decided to cooperate.

I laughed. "You don't need to worry about your grandmother, Larry. She's having the time of her life."

Mags sat next to him and patted his arm. "If anyone can handle those agents, it's her."

"What are y'all up to? I'm sure it won't be on Davis's approved list." Larry chuckled, his shoulders easing from their raised position.

"Probably not," I said, "but he can't very well investigate while he's accompanying Tweedle Dee and Tweedle Dum down a dead end."

"You three go eat," Mags said. "I've got some candy in my purse. I'm going to stay with Larry."

"Sweetie." He planted a tender kiss on her cheek.

I wanted to say we'd stay, too, but the growl of my stomach gave me away. "We'll get a doggy bag for you two and meet at the house later."

"Thanks." Larry returned his attention to the short hallway where the interrogation room was.

"How about pizza?" Eric suggested. "We can order one for them to share and it'll be easy to warm up."

"That's my man. Always thinking." I linked my arm with his as we returned to his jeep. Eating before going to the bar would allow me to come up with a line of questioning instead of blurting out whatever came to my mind. "Ann, can you pull up driver's license photos of the Wilsons?"

"Already saved in my gallery."

Of course she knew how to do her job. She definitely didn't need me telling her how.

We chose a corner booth near the window of the pizza parlor and placed our order. Once the waitress had left, I asked, "Should we tell Pat a couple of my residents have disappeared and we wonder if he's seen them? Then if he denies it, I can show him the coaster."

"That's as good an idea as any," Eric said, "but it'll be easy for him to say too many people go in and out of there for him to remember them all."

"We can also ask about Mrs. Acres and Jose. Ann

is good at reading body language—" Of course, I was developing the skill, too. "—and she can judge his reaction to my questions."

"Why not let me do the questioning?" Ann asked. "I'm the one with the PI license. You can say you've hired me in an official capacity to find your missing tenants."

"Good idea." I lifted my hand for a high-five.

She grinned and slapped her hand against mine. "I'm paid to ask questions. Maybe he'll be less suspicious."

"Have you done a background check?" Eric glanced in the rearview mirror.

"Yes. I like to be prepared. Nothing more serious than a DUI two years ago."

The atmosphere around the bar and Jose's restaurant seemed as thick as a heavy fog. Glares from the young people hanging on street corners sent chills down my spine. We were not wanted, and I doubted anyone would be giving us any clues on this visit.

"I don't think my jeep is safe here," Eric said.

"Park right out front and set your alarm," Ann advised. "You can keep an eye on it from the front door."

Heads turned and people frowned as we entered the bar. Jose's table sat empty, draped with a black tablecloth. He might have been a crook, but he'd been nice to me and left me the map. That alone caused me to feel some loyalty for the man.

"We should have brought flowers," I said.

"Are you serious?" Ann hissed. "Jose would have killed you the moment he no longer needed you."

"He gave me the map," I whispered.

"Quiet." Eric took up a position near the door, leaving me to follow Ann to where a scowling Pat served drinks.

We squeezed in an opening at the end and ordered two sparkling waters. Pat rolled his eyes.

"Here to gloat?" He slapped down two bottles.

"To mourn, actually," I said. "Jose and I shared respect for each other." Some of the hate eased on the faces of those around us. "But we are here for another reason, too."

Ann showed him her phone screen and badge. "Have you seen these two people?"

"No, why?" He glanced at the screen, then wiped vigorously at a spot on the bar.

"They're tenants of Miss Turley and they're missing."

"Ain't seen 'em. You can ask around if you want." He moved to serve another customer.

I slid the coaster toward him. "They were here at least once."

He narrowed his eyes. "Look. I can't remember every face unless they're regulars. Get it? I'm sorry if they're missing." The hard glint in his eyes said he wasn't. "Now, this is a wake for Jose. So either buy a drink or leave."

"They arrested someone," Ann said. "An old woman. Do you remember her?"

"Dolled up like she was going to church on Sunday with a hat and white gloves? Yeah, not someone a person can forget." He crossed his arms, revealing bulging muscles through his tee shirt.

"Did you see whether she spoke with Jose?"

He shook his head. "I was in the alley."

"Where Jose was killed" I pointed out.

"What are you saying?" His face darkened. "You accusing me of killing him?"

"We aren't accusing you of anything," Ann said. "We're just trying to piece some things together."

"Why? You ain't the cops." He sneered.

"I'm sure you know how nosy my friend is." Ann gave a thin-lipped smile. "She's worried about her tenants and sad about Jose. We want answers."

"I don't have any."

Catching sight of the waitress, cocktail girl— whatever role she played at the bar—ducking into the women's restroom, I excused myself and rushed after her. Before opening the door, I nodded at Ann to stay where she was. It would be suspicious if we both went to the restroom. We weren't in middle school.

Since the woman was in a stall, I entered the one next to her, exiting a few seconds after she did. When I joined her at the sink, she was redoing her bright red lipstick.

"Sad about Jose, huh?" I washed my hands.

Tears sparkled in her eyes. "Yes," she said with a thick Hispanic accent. "He was a good man."

Questionable, but I'd go with it. "Do you think the old woman killed him?"

She shrugged one shoulder and blotted her lips with a piece of tissue. "Why would she? An old woman is no threat to a man like Jose. If you have a desire to be killed, you should be questioning his enemies."

"Also dead." I studied her through the mirror.

"Unless you know the phantom third man."

"I don't." She frowned. "I've got to get back to work. Be careful. These people don't like too many questions asked."

"You do know all the things Jose was involved in, don't you? Drugs, trafficking, theft—"

"He was good to me. That is what matters." She tossed the tissue with a perfectly formed imprint of her lips into the trash can. "Adios." She hurried from the restroom.

I retrieved the tissue, folded it, and slipped it into my pocket. Loyalty seemed strong in Jose's employ. We needed to find the three men Mrs. Acres had watched in the woods. Maybe Shante could help. First, we'd have to find him, and I had no idea where to look. How dangerous would it be to wander the streets asking questions if people thought me a friend of Jose's?

I rejoined Ann at the bar where a drunk man did his best to flirt with her and ended up looking like an overeager teenager. Ann's cool demeanor would be hard for anyone to crack but next to impossible for someone she looked at with scorn.

Pat kept shooting glances our way but didn't come to refresh our water. Since the bar was filled to capacity, I figured he was too busy.

"Ready to go?" I asked Ann.

"More than ready." She peeled the drunk's hand off her arm.

Outside, I broached the idea of asking some questions. "You're armed, right?"

Ann nodded. "I'm not sure it's a good idea."

"At least let me talk to the same group of boys

that gave me Jose's name."

"I'll drive alongside you," Eric said. "I'm not risking my jeep. This way, we can make a fast getaway if we need to."

Ann didn't look happy about the situation but gave a reluctant nod. "Don't walk away from me."

"I won't." I set off down the sidewalk in the direction I'd spotted the group.

Wariness crossed the boys' faces as we approached, especially when they realized Eric drove alongside us. I pasted on a grin. "I'm looking for someone."

"Anybody like you who comes here is looking for someone or something." The oldest one of the group sneered. "You cops?"

"Private investigator." Ann flashed her badge. "I have no authority to arrest anyone. We're looking for some missing people." She showed them the photo of the Wilsons.

The young man glanced at his buddies. "They went to the restaurant a lot."

It had to have been often for him to remember them. "Do you know anyone named Shante Leroy?"

"Worked for Jacobson." He narrowed his eyes. "Why do you want him?"

"Questions." I smiled. "You're answering easy today. Why?"

"All the bosses are dead." He laughed. "We're our own now. Freedom has a great taste."

"Rumor has it there's a new guy trying to make a name for himself."

His smile faded. "You heard that, too?"

I nodded. "Talked to Jose about it. He didn't

know who. Do you?"

"No, but maybe we shouldn't be talking. I let the fresh air of freedom cloud my judgment."

"Do you know where Shante lives?" I held my breath.

"One of those motels on the highway that rents by the week. The pink one." He motioned with his head for his friends to follow him down the street.

Our conversation might be over, but we'd learned a lot. A third person was known on the streets and we had a place to start looking for Shante. I grinned at Ann. "Guess what we're doing tomorrow?" A ride up the mountain could wait another day. We were getting close to solving the case. I could feel it in my gut.

Chapter Twenty-one

The next morning, I woke much earlier than I needed to. The excitement of feeling we were close to ending months of crime invigorated me. Caper jumped off the bed and tore down the stairs to the front door. I tossed off the blankets and followed her, waiting on the porch while she did her business.

Eric's shadow passed behind the drawn blinds of his window. Someone else couldn't sleep in either.

"I'd like to sleep in one morning when I work with you." Ann grumbled and thrust a cup of coffee into my hands.

"Thank you. Sorry, I've never been one to sleep late."

"Obviously." She sipped her coffee.

My gaze roamed the grounds, pleased to see a light on in Mrs. Acres' house. I hope she put the agents in their place. Ridiculous to think she could kill a man like Jose.

Mags stepped out of her front door, locked it, and made her way to us. "Since you're up, I guess we'll be leaving at this ungodly hour. The sun is barely up."

"The earlier we knock on Shante's door, the more likely we'll get there before he leaves." I grinned around the rim of my cup. "All I need to do is get dressed and let Eric know we're ready."

"Coffee?"

"I'll get it." Ann moved back inside.

"Larry got his grandmother home?" I asked.

Mags nodded. "They couldn't hold her on the fact she'd gone to the bar. Even they need more proof than that. Besides, she told them she was an alcoholic and frequented bars at all hours of the day."

I laughed. "They believed her?"

"I doubt it, but she thought it funny. Said their faces turned beet red, but they kept their composure." Mags grinned. "I'm starting to like her."

"Me, too. Before she came, you were the most colorful character at Heavenly Acres."

"Oh, honey, I still am." She turned to accept a travel mug of coffee from Ann. "I guess we're leaving."

"I've more thermoses," Ann said. "Get Eric and let's go talk to Shante."

I gave her a salute and went to knock on Eric's door. "Ready?" I asked when he answered.

"Yep, and I'm taking Hershey. No more going to a shady part of town without my guard dog. She can keep watch over the jeep." He whistled, and Hershey darted down the steps. "I hate leaving him home all the time."

I glanced at my house. "Caper wouldn't be much help at a hotel. She'll have to stay put until we head up the mountain. On second thought, we could leave her in the jeep with Hershey."

"Whatever you want. It isn't as if she takes up a lot of room."

I smiled and hurried home to put a leash on my dog and change into some yoga pants and a tee shirt.

Less than an hour later, we pulled into the parking lot of a motel that might have once been classified as pink. Now the stucco walls were more a shade of faded peach.

"Wait here," Ann said. "I'll check with the manager to see whether Shante has rented a room." She climbed from the jeep and disappeared into the front office. A few minutes later, she waved for us to join her. "Room 202," she said. "The manager said he believes Shante is still here because he drives that beat-up Chevy."

I glanced to where a car sat parked next to the stairs leading to the second floor. I glanced upward, counting the doors. The second one from the stairs hung open a few inches. "Something's wrong."

The others followed my gaze. Ann pulled her gun and led the way upstairs. "Stay behind me," she said. "Away from the window."

We plastered our backs against the wall between 202 and 203 while Ann slowly pushed open the door to Shante's room. "Shante Leroy? Private Investigator Ann Lowery. I'd like to ask you some questions."

A moan came from inside. Ann shot me a worried look and slipped into the room, the rest of us on her heels.

A pair of gym shoe-covered feet stuck out from

between two queen-size beds. I ran over to see Shante lying in a pool of blood from a gunshot wound to the shoulder.

"I'll check the bathroom." Ann darted away. "Window's open and room is empty," she called.

"I'll call an ambulance," Eric said.

I knelt next to Shante and yanked a pillowcase off a pillow. Pressing it to his wound, I asked, "Do you know who did this?"

"Masked. Get. My. Pants."

It was then I noticed he lay there in his boxers and a tee-shirt. Cold-hearted to shoot a man in his underwear.

Mags tossed me his pants. "Does he want us to get him dressed?"

"No, keys."

She dug in the pockets until she located a ring of keys. "Now what?"

"Briefcase. Top shelf. Closet."

She rushed to grab the briefcase and set it on the bed.

Shante pushed my hands away and struggled to a sitting position. "Contact Davis." His arms trembled as he pushed to his feet. He sat on the edge of the bed and unlocked the briefcase. Reaching inside, he pulled out a locked box, unlocked it and tossed me a badge. "Undercover, Julian Drew." He fell backward.

"Davis said no ambulance," Ann said. "He wants us to take the detective straight to the ER and ask for Doctor Ryan. We cannot let the detective's true identity be known."

"But who shot him?" My eyes widened. I

grabbed another pillowcase and formed a makeshift bandage for his shoulder, tying one around the other to keep it in place.

"We'll find out later," Eric said. "Let's go. I've already called the ambulance." He propped his shoulder under Drew while Ann led the way onto the balcony.

From the jeep, Hershey and Caper set up a fit of barking. Ann pushed us back into the room. "Whoever shot the detective may still be out there. Lock yourselves in. Don't open the door for anyone but me."

"The ambulance," I said.

"Try canceling." She opened the door and hurried out.

Julian would bleed to death at this rate. "How long ago were you shot?"

"Minutes before you arrived." He sagged into a chair. "We cannot stay here."

I agreed. "We've got to get to the jeep. Hopefully, the barking and Ann chased the shooter away from here."

Eric helped Julian back to his feet. I yanked open the door and we rushed out, making our way down the stairs to the jeep without incident. Eric crowded Julian in with the dogs and Mags. "We've got to find Ann."

"There." I pointed to where Ann raced around the corner of the building.

In the distance, sirens wailed. A wide-eyed man watched from the office window. Talk about creating a commotion. We'd done everything but get in and out quietly.

Eric laid on the horn until Ann raced back toward us. She dove into the jeep, and we sped away.

"Hold on, Julian," I said, gripping the dashboard and Eric veered onto the street.

Bullets pinged the back of the jeep.

"Why can't I have a car that isn't shot up?" Eric glared in the rearview mirror. "Masked man. One guess as to who he wants."

"Never mind that. Julian is bleeding badly," Mags said. "Get us to the hospital."

It was at least twenty minutes away. All we could do at that point was pray and break the speed limit.

"Who would be able to find out you were undercover?" I turned in my seat to Julian.

"He's lost consciousness," Ann said. "We'll have to ask questions later."

At the hospital, Ann rushed inside to get a wheelchair. When she returned, we helped Eric get the unconscious man on the chair. "Doctor Ryan must be a code word," Ann said, "because no one asked any questions. Just told me to take the patient past admissions to ER room number four."

Clever way of getting undercover detectives the medical attention they needed without giving away their identity. "Is Davis going to meet us here?"

"I'm already here." He stepped from the curtains of number four.

Two nurses took over and whisked Julian away, saying someone would be out to speak with us after his surgery.

I had so many questions, but Davis said this wasn't the place. After Julian's surgery, he'd be taken to a room under guard. We could talk there. He led us to the private room and closed the door.

"Who's going to guard him?" I asked.

"Milton. He's the only one I trust."

"You don't trust the agents?"

"They don't seem to be working overly hard at finding Jose's killer. They seem more concerned about finding the tunnels. I find that suspicious."

Could it be they were behind it all? "My thoughts are leaning toward Pat, the bartender."

"There are several people working behind the scenes here," Davis said, sitting in a green vinyl chair. "I'm only speculating at this point."

"Maybe the agents are focusing on the tunnels because they think that is the answer to all the questions," Ann said. "It makes sense."

I nodded. "Find the tunnels. Find out the motives for the crime. Find the person responsible." It'd been my plan, but I kept getting sidetracked.

"I can't keep the dogs in the car," Eric said. "How about I take them home, then pick up lunch for us all? The detective will be in surgery for a few hours."

"That sounds like a great plan," I said.

Two hours later, our stomachs were full of burgers and fries, and Julian was brought to us from recovery.

"He'll be fine after a few days," the doctor said. "He lost a lot of blood, but whoever tied those pillowcases together most likely saved his life."

A rush of pride flooded through me. I'd always been able to use my head in a crisis.

Julian's eyes flickered open.

"Glad you made it." I smiled.

His mouth twitched. "Glad y'all decided to visit."

"We had no idea who you were. We wanted to question you about Jose and the men you saw at Heavenly Acres."

"Who saw me there?" He frowned.

"Mrs. Acres," we said in unison.

"You don't look old enough to be a detective," I said.

"I'm older than I look."

"That's why Detective Drew makes such a good gangster," Davis said. "His baby face can fool almost anyone."

"I can't believe you kept this a secret." I frowned.

"I couldn't take the chance of his identity being found out. As it is, someone guessed. I'd like to know how."

Julian shook his head. "No, I was shot because I was caught snooping around. If the shooter had known my identity, they would have searched the room and found my ID. Instead, they shot me and left shortly before y'all pulled up."

"Was the man who shot you one of the ones you saw in the woods?" Ann asked.

"The build was the same." Julian's eyes started to drift closed. "You should leave this one to the authorities, ladies."

So I'd been told many times. Still, it had been my actions that caught the bad guys in the past. I intended for that to happen again. "There's no one left for us to question. We've already spoken to the bartender. That was a dead-end."

"Not so—" Julian fell asleep.

"You got more out of him today then I thought you would," Davis said. "I expected him to be pretty incoherent when brought to the room. Go home and stay out of trouble."

"Yes, sir." I grinned.

He rolled his eyes. "Don't tell me what you're planning. My head hurts just thinking about it."

"We know the drill," Mags said. "Call you when we know something or need saving."

Chapter Twenty-two

I woke early the next morning but not as early as Ann. Not seeing her downstairs, I stepped onto the porch to see her talking to a good-looking man in his early to mid-thirties. Grinning, I skipped down the steps.

"Good morning," I sang, thrusting out my hand. "CJ Turley."

"Scott Mane." He glanced at Ann as he returned my shake.

"Oh, all right." She sighed. "CJ, this is my contact. Yes, we're seeing each other."

He laughed. "At least we try to. The mishaps CJ's always getting into makes it difficult."

I wrinkled my nose. "Did you bring us new information?"

"Nope. Was passing by on my way to work and wanted to say hello to Ann." His warm gaze gave me hope she might finally find happiness. "Be careful," he said softly.

"I will." She beamed and walked him to his car.

When she returned, my grin widened. "He's cute."

She laughed. "Yes, he is. Let's get this day started."

Back in the house, we packed sandwiches and chips for lunch, water bottles and soda for drinks, and some snacks for us and the dogs. Since Larry and Mags thought it best we take two vehicles so we could cover more ground, we had room in the side-by-side for Hershey and Caper. I was glad. The dogs made a good warning system.

By the time we finished gathering what we thought we'd need for the day, Eric, Larry, and Mags waited for us outside.

Larry glanced over at me. "You ready?"

I nodded. "I'm hoping it isn't a wasted trip."

"Be careful." He gave a small smile. "You're the only family I've got." He hit the gas and shot forward.

"They're taking the east side," Eric said. "We'll take the west. We've got walkie-talkies and trackers on our phones." He handed Ann and me a radio. "Channel four. Keep it with you at all times, but do try not to get separated." He gave me a quick kiss to let me know he was just speaking to me.

I gave him a playful punch to the shoulder and climbed into the vehicle with Caper on my lap. With Hershey and Ann in the back seat, there wasn't much room even for a small dog. Seconds later, we were speeding away from the community and up the mountain.

Please, let us find the tunnels so this could all end.

Not only were their dead crime bosses, but someone had tried to add Shante, I mean, Julian, to the list of deaths. Since Caper hadn't found anymore drugs, and Mrs. Acres hadn't reported anymore strangers poking around, I assumed nothing more was buried on the property. That left the mountain to answer the rest of our questions.

If not for the seriousness of our plans for the day, I'd have enjoyed the ride. The early morning sun kissed the ground through the branches of the trees. Squirrels chased each other across our path. A doe and her fawn leaped into the brush as we approached. A perfect summer morning with what might be an approaching storm, literally.

Clouds built in the distance. "Is rain in the forecast? I didn't bring any ponchos."

"I did," Ann said. "But, no, it isn't supposed to rain, but we know how reliable the weather is."

I glanced at the tarp roof and hoped it would hold against a summer downpour. There was nothing more miserable than being wet.

Paper rustled behind me and I turned to see Ann studying a copy of the map Larry had printed off. "Find a place to pull over," she said. "Those rocks look promising."

I glanced to where a pile of boulders leaned precariously against each other. We'd be looking for an opening or a cave.

"The entrance won't be easy to find," Eric said. "Keep Caper on a leash so she doesn't disappear. If you find something that might be what we're looking for, let me check it out. We don't want to startle a bear or a cougar."

No, we did not. Since Eric was the park ranger and used to the woods, I was more than happy to step back and let him take charge. The first pile of boulders revealed nothing more than a shelter that looked like it would make a nice hiding place for snakes. No thank you.

I stepped back and studied the area. The entrance to tunnels used for nefarious means wouldn't look like a typical entrance. It'd be disguised, made to look like something it wasn't.

I stepped through a natural rock arch and stared over a bluff into a creek. "I found the perfect place for a picnic." Large flagstones made a smooth surface next to the water.

Thunder rumbled in the distance. Hopefully, the rain would go around us. "Maybe we should eat in case it rains."

Since it was close to noon, the others agreed, and we made our way down a steep embankment to the water's edge. We found large rocks to sit on, and I passed out our lunch, studying the area around us as we ate. "Does this area get many visitors?"

"Not that I know of," Eric said. "Why?"

"Look down the creek bed. The flagstone down there seems to have been placed there on purpose to form a bridge." My gaze followed it up the side we'd climbed down. "It's also not as steep over there." I scrambled to my feet.

"Stay where I can see you," Eric said.

I nodded and took a bite of my sandwich as I walked. Yep. Tire tracks of the four-wheel variety. "I think I found a crossing." The question now was which way to the tunnel entrance? Did the path lead across the creek or to where we were?

The other two joined me. "We can waste the rest of the day if we head in the wrong direction," Ann said.

"Let me do some scouting." Eric called for Hershey. "You two stay here. Don't leave. I want to be able to find you so we can move quickly if we need to."

"Be careful." I put a hand on his arm. "If the bad guys are out there—"

"I'm going on foot to be quieter." He kissed me. "You stay out of sight if you can. Someone riding by will see you if you're by the water. Wait under that overhang for me. If it does rain, you'll be dry."

"What about the side-by-side?"

"Nothing I can do about it but throw a camouflage tarp over it and hope for the best." He climbed up the embankment, pushed the vehicle into the bushes, and covered it up. With a wink, he jogged toward the rock bridge and across the creek.

I sat under the overhang and hugged my knees as the day cooled. "I hope he's back soon. I don't do well with inactivity."

"No, you don't," Ann agreed. "Boredom tends to get you in trouble."

The far-off roar of an engine broke the silence. I hoped it was Larry and Mags and not the bad guys. We were sitting targets here, overhang or not.

"We should have stayed together. What if Eric finds the entrance? What if he doesn't? Working together would increase our chances."

"Why don't you wander around here, staying out of sight. Maybe you'll get lucky. Caper seems to be enjoying herself." Ann motioned to where Caper sniffed around a bush.

Following my dog around had to be better than doing nothing but worry about Eric. I pushed to my feet and joined Caper. "Don't you dare dig up a snake."

Caper's answer was a fast tail wag before moving to a large rock that sort of resembled a triangle with a rounded point. I stood and followed it upward with my gaze before glancing at my feet.

A copperhead slithered inches in front of my toes. I froze, not breathing, not making a sound until it disappeared into the bushes. A scream burst forth despite a hand clapped over my mouth.

Ann shot to her feet. "What is it?"

"A snake." I shuddered, then froze again as birds burst from the trees because of my scream. Anyone within a mile around us would know someone was in the woods. "I'm sorry, but snakes terrify me."

"Yes, I know." Ann stood still and stared into the thick trees across the creek. Then, she turned to where the snake had come from. "Does that rock look strange to you?"

"I was studying it when the snake slithered past." It practically sat flush against the rock wall behind it. Being careful to watch where I placed my foot, I peered around the rock. Some things could be deceiving. Rather than lean against the wall, the triangular rock hid a crevice. "I think I've found the entrance."

Ann took a look. "Which means, they cross their vehicles at the creek, but most likely walk in the water to cover their tracks. That way, they don't appear to be anything more than folks out enjoying the day. They meaning the bad guys."

"I got that." I wasn't that dense.

Something crashed through the brush.

Ann drew her gun.

Eric darted across the creek, Hershey on his heels. "Up to the side-by-side. Now!"

He didn't have to tell us twice. I scooped Caper into my arms and started climbing.

At the top, Eric tore off the tarp. We climbed in and he sent us shooting glance back in the direction we'd come.

"Who screamed?" He asked.

"I saw a snake." I grabbed a strap used as a handle. "Were you being chased?"

"I was watching two men unload some packages from the back of a four-wheeler. They turned when you screamed. I couldn't duck fast enough. They gave chase. Here we are."

Running for our lives. Again. "I'm sorry."

He squeezed my hand. "You couldn't help it. Let's just hope they don't catch up to us. Ann, alert Larry and Mags, please. We aren't alone out here."

"We found the entrance," I said, smiling despite the direness of our situation.

"Good job."

Ann radioed Larry. "I also texted Davis that we found what we believe to be the entrance to the tunnels."

"It is the entrance." I scowled over my shoulder.

"We haven't gone in to verify that."

Ever practical Ann. I yelped as Eric took a corner fast and grabbed Caper before she slid off my lap.

"Why not head straight down?"

"They'll expect that. I want them to think we went down, but now we're going east."

The roar of an engine had us turning again. "Maybe we should have run on foot. If we can hear them, they can hear us." My heart leaped into my throat.

"We'll be okay." Eric shot me a quick glance. "Davis has a relatively good idea of where we are. Larry and Mags can track us—"

"My text failed to send," Ann said. "There's no service up here. Davis has no idea where we are."

Two four-wheelers emerged from the trees in front of us. Two masked men aimed weapons at us.

Eric braked to a stop.

Ann drew her gun.

One of the men fired.

She fell off the back of the side-by-side.

"Ann!"

Hershey and Caper started barking.

"You two are coming with us," one of the men said.

Ann made a small movement without opening her eyes. "Leave the dogs," she whispered. "I'm hit, but not fatally. I'll need the dogs to find you."

Eric and I pushed the dogs out of the vehicle as one of the four-wheelers circled around behind us. I closed my eyes and prayed the man wouldn't shoot Ann again.

Chapter Twenty-three

Our captors led us back to the creek, and as I'd deduced, marched us through the water and into the crevice. I caught sight of Caper running along the bluff's edge, only to have something, or someone, call her back. I prayed it had been Ann and not a bear.

Although they'd secured Eric's hands with zip ties, they'd left mine free. They must not have believed me to be much of a threat. That only meant they didn't know me. I was fury in a tiny package and wanted justice for them shooting Ann. Please, God, don't let her die. I wasn't paying her to protect me this time. I'd hate for her to die doing me a favor.

"You okay?" Eric spoke from behind me.

"Yes, you?"

"Fine."

"No talking." From the grunt I heard, the man must have jabbed Eric with his gun. "The boss isn't going to be pleased y'all were snooping around."

They squeezed us through the crevice into a surprising well-constructed tunnel. Dirt-packed walls that had stood for centuries if the vines crisscrossing through were any indication. Here and there wooden beams helped support the dirt above us. Still, my blood ran cold at the thought of being buried alive if the tunnel collapsed.

I fought to regulate my breathing. I wasn't prone to anxiety attacks, but I recognized the start of one. Breathe, CJ. In and out, in and out, slowly.

"Stop." Eric moved to my side. "What's wrong?"

"I. Can't. Be. In. Here."

"Stop the drama." I got poked for my trouble and glanced up to see Pat the bartender strolling toward us.

"Don't like the underground?" He smirked. "Pick up the pace."

"You're the one trying to take over." I squared my shoulders and willed away the anxiety. It didn't work. My heart still skipped erratically, and my breathing came quicker than it should. I reached out to touch Eric, drawing strength from the feel of him.

We followed Pat into a widened area of the tunnel where boxes were stacked. Yep, the tunnels were perfect for smuggling drugs and anything else a person wanted. A table in the middle of the room sat stacked high with bags of white powder, scales, and Ziploc baggies.

"I do appreciate you keeping the FBI and local law enforcement occupied while I established my authority here," Pat said. "It will take a while to build up the army I want to help me, but I'm a patient man."

"I had nothing to do with you." I scowled. "We've all known there was a third person involved.

That's who everyone has been looking for."

"Wasn't it clever of me to pit the Jacobsons and Rivera against each other?" He grinned. "I've had so much fun. Alas, now it all must end." He waved a hand. "Dispose of them, Jones. I've an empire to build." He motioned for the man who kept poking us to follow him.

Jones, the one who had remained quiet during our stroll through the tunnels, motioned his rifle. "Against the wall." He glanced in the direction the other two had gone, then turning back to us, pulled a knife from his pocket and cut Eric's bindings. "I'm undercover. Hit me in the back of the head with something, Miss Turley. It has to look as if you surprised me."

I glanced around not seeing even a rock. "With what?" No one would believe I could knock him out with a punch.

A curse bellowed down the tunnel.

Jones whirled. "Run."

Eric grabbed my hand and yanked me after him.

A gunshot rang out.

As we rounded a corner, I glanced back to see Jones fall. My gaze met an enraged Pat before Eric pulled me along.

Our feet pounded the packed dirt. When we reached the crevice, Eric shoved me through, then followed. "The opposite way." He pushed me up the bank across the creek. "Don't look back. Keep running. Our lives depend on it."

With the occasional shove against my rear by Eric, I made it to the top. Pat and his sidekick scrambled after us. At least they couldn't shoot us while climbing. Eric grabbed my hand, and we continued our mad dash through the Ozark mountain forest.

I wanted to ask where we were going, where we would hide, but Eric seemed to have a destination in mind. Talking while sprinting would have been more than even I, a master of talking, could accomplish.

Somewhere behind us, a dog barked. Not Caper. Deeper, like Hershey. Did that mean Ann was alive or dead? Were the dogs alone in the woods without a human? I tried looking back only to have Eric spur me on.

My legs burned, my breath came in gasps, and still we ran, Pat and the other man gaining on us. I thanked God for the thick underbrush that kept the gunmen from getting a clear shot at us. It made fleeing difficult but probably saved our lives.

Eric stopped on a bluff overlooking a river and held out his hand. "Do you trust me?"

"Are we jumping?" Oh, God.

He nodded. "Do you trust me?"

"Of course, I do." I glanced back at the sound of crashing through the brush and put my hand in his.

"Will you marry me?"

"What?" My eyes widened.

"If we survive this, will you marry me?"

"If?" I squeaked.

He jumped, pulling me with him.

I shouted yes an instant before submerging in the river. I popped up to see Pat on the bluff taking aim and dove under. The bullet sliced the water next to me. I kicked my feet, then let the water carry me along, surfacing when my lungs screamed for air.

"Eric?" I glanced around me, hoping, praying for a glimpse of him.

"Here." He hung over a low-hanging branch and reached for me.

I missed and continued downstream. Was that a waterfall I heard? I stopped flailing my arms and legs as if by doing so, I'd stop my rush toward the falls, if there was one. This was it. I know I'd said it before, but now I knew how I would die. In a sodden lump after falling over a waterfall.

"If you go over, keep your arms and legs tight," Eric called out from behind me.

"Why did you jump back in the water?" I started swimming again, trying to reach the bank. The current was too strong, and I was swept over. I plastered my arms to my sides, my legs together, and held my breath.

I bounced off the bottom of the pool I landed in, swallowed a mouthful of water so cold it made my teeth hurt, and grinned. I'd made it. I was alive. The calmer water of the pool made it easy to swim to shore. On the bank, I lay there and gasped for air like a stranded fish, letting the warm sun stop my shivers.

Eric crawled up beside me. "Did you say yes?"

"Of course, I did." I turned my head to face him.

He grinned. "I thought I might have imagined it."

A bullet pinged off a nearby boulder.

"Darn." Eric scrambled to his feet. "I thought we'd lost them by jumping."

Pat and the other man stood at the top of the falls.

"I guess we can keep moving. Eventually we'll run into Davis or the agents and they can take over." Wishful thinking on my part?

We resumed our dash through the woods. I hoped Eric knew where we were because I'd grown hopelessly lost. We emerged from the brush onto a dirt road. "Can we follow this out?"

"We could," Eric said, "but those men will too. We have to stay in the brush."

"Do you know where we are?" I took advantage of the lull in our race to catch my breath.

"Sort of." He flashed a grin and off we went again. The man was a machine.

"Wait. Hear that?" I stopped, straining my ears. "There. An engine. Larry?"

"I sure hope so." We followed the sound.

I jumped up and down at the sight of Larry and Mags coming over a hill. Larry stopped, we hopped on, and he sped off down the road.

Mags turned in her seat. "I told Larry it would be like a needle in the haystack finding the two of you. I was wrong. Why are you wet?"

"We jumped over a cliff, and we're getting married." Eric cupped my face and kissed me.

I returned his kiss with passion, thrilled to be alive with my man, although we may not be out of danger yet.

"Married?" Mags clapped her hands. "You two have a story to tell. Ann is waiting down the road with Davis."

"She's okay?" I pulled away from Eric.

"Shot in the arm, but she'll live."

"The dogs?"

Her smile faded. "There's no sign of them. Ann said they took off after you when you were taken."

Eric patted my arm. "Hershey will find her way

and bring Caper with her."

"I hope so." I loved my adventurous pup. She kept life interesting with her games and tendency to get me into trouble.

"Hold on." Larry sped up a hill and off the road as Pat and the other man darted from the trees. They shot at us, their shots wild.

"At least they're still following us." I kept my gaze on them until we pulled too far ahead.

At the bottom of the mountain, Davis, Milton, and the FBI agents donned Kevlar vests. Ann sat on a fallen log, her arm wrapped in a white cloth. Davis must have gotten help from other police departments because it looked like a small army.

Ann smiled, seeing us. "I can't wait to hear how you got away."

"An undercover agent," I said, sliding from the vehicle. "I'm pretty sure he gave his life for us."

"Do you need medical attention?" Davis asked. When I shook my head, he said, "then I'll see you at your house later to get your statement."

"I'm not leaving until I find my dog." Tears welled in my eyes.

"Staying here could get you killed."

"If I'm not here and you don't find Pat, he'll come to my house. I'm in danger wherever I am until he's caught." My gaze caught sight of a crazy-eyed Pat on top of the hill. "There!"

Guns raised to shoot.

"No." Eric darted forward as Hershey latched onto Pat's arm. "Don't hit my dog."

The man's shrieks could be heard from where we stood. Caper's shrill barks joined the ruckus, although I couldn't see her. Where was the other man?

Davis whirled and fired behind me.

I turned to see the other gunman fall.

Milton fired at Pat's feet.

Hershey released him and darted into the trees.

Law enforcement opened fire.

I folded to the ground next to Ann. "Eric and I are getting married."

"When did this happen?"

"As we jumped off a cliff into a river."

I laughed as Hershey and Caper, tongues lolling, galloped toward us. I scooped my dog into my arms and met Eric's warm gaze over her head. "I hope you won't be bored married to a woman who has sworn off sticking her nose in other people's business."

He laughed so hard he staggered backward.

"It isn't that funny." I frowned.

"Sweetheart, when you stop being nosy, that will be the day I buy a farm, and I don't like farming."

I rolled my eyes but couldn't keep my smile from returning when he sat next to me, one arm around me, the other around Hershey. Both dogs were as filthy as we were, and my arms sported scrapes and scratches. No matter. We were still breathing. I leaned my head against Eric's shoulder. "I love you."

"Ditto, baby."

The End

Check out the next book, Caper Steals
Christmas by scanning this code.

Dear Reader,

I hope you enjoyed this mystery as much as I
loved writing it. Isn't CJ just the luckiest woman to
have Eric who loves her even though she gets him
in danger? He'd do almost anything for her. If you
enjoyed *A Strange Game for Caper*, please leave a
review. Reviews are very important to an author. I
look forward to seeing you in another adventure.

Cynthia

Website at www.cynthiahickey.com

Multi-published and Amazon and ECPA Best-Selling author Cynthia Hickey has sold close to a million copies of her works since 2013. She has taught a Continuing Education class at the 2015 American Christian Fiction Writers conference, several small ACFW chapters and RWA chapters, and small writer retreats. She and her husband run the small press, Winged Publications, which includes some of the CBA's best well-known authors. She lives in Arizona and Arkansas, becoming a snowbird, with her husband and one dog. She has ten grandchildren who keep her busy and tell everyone they know that "Nana is a writer".

Connect with me on FaceBook
Twitter
Bookbub
Sign up for my newsletter and receive a free short story
www.cynthiahickey.com

Follow me on Amazon

Enjoy other books by Cynthia Hickey

Brothers Steele
Sharp as Steele
Carved in Steele
Forged in Steele
Brothers Steele (All three in one)

Fantasy
Fate of the Faes
Shayna
Deema
Kasdeya

Time Travel
The Portal

Tiny House Mysteries
No Small Caper
Caper Goes Missing
Caper Finds a Clue
Caper's Dark Adventure
A Strange Game for Caper

Wife for Hire – Private Investigators
Saving Sarah
Lesson for Lacey
Mission for Meghan
Long Way for Lainie
Aimed at Amy
Wife for Hire (all five in one)

A Hollywood Murder

Killer Pose, book 1
Killer Snapshot, book 2
Shoot to Kill, book 3
Kodak Kill Shot, book 4
To Snap a Killer
Hollywood Murder Mysteries

Shady Acres Mysteries
Beware the Orchids, book 1
Path to Nowhere
Poison Foliage
Poinsettia Madness
Deadly Greenhouse Gases
Vine Entrapment

CLEAN BUT GRITTY Romantic Suspense

Highland Springs

Murder Live
Say Bye to Mommy
To Breathe Again
Highland Springs Murders (all 3 in one)

Colors of Evil Series

Shades of Crimson
Coral Shadows

The Pretty Must Die Series

Ripped in Red, book 1

Pierced in Pink, book 2
Wounded in White, book 3
Worthy, The Complete Story

Lisa Paxton Mystery Series

Eenie Meenie Miny Mo
Jack Be Nimble
Hickory Dickory Dock

A Heart of Valor
The Game
Suspicious Minds
After the Storm
Local Betrayal

Overcoming Evil series
Mistaken Assassin
Captured Innocence
Mountain of Fear
Exposure at Sea
A Secret to Die for
Collision Course
Romantic Suspense of 5 books in 1

INSPIRATIONAL

Whisper Sweet Nothings (a short romance)

Nosy Neighbor Series
Anything For A Mystery, Book 1
A Killer Plot, Book 2
Skin Care Can Be Murder, Book 3
Death By Baking, Book 4
Jogging Is Bad For Your Health, Book 5
Poison Bubbles, Book 6
A Good Party Can Kill You, Book 7 (Final)
Nosy Neighbor collection

Christmas with Stormi Nelson

The Summer Meadows Series
Fudge-Laced Felonies, Book 1
Candy-Coated Secrets, Book 2
Chocolate-Covered Crime, Book 3
Maui Macadamia Madness, Book 4
All four novels in one collection

The River Valley Mystery Series
Deadly Neighbors, Book 1
Advance Notice, Book 2
The Librarian's Last Chapter, Book 3
All three novels in one collection

Historical cozy
Hazel's Quest

Historical Romances
Runaway Sue

Taming the Sheriff
Sweet Apple Blossom
A Doctor's Agreement
A Lady Maid's Honor
A Touch of Sugar
Love Over Par
Heart of the Emerald

Finding Love the Harvey Girl Way
Cooking With Love
Guiding With Love
Serving With Love
Warring With Love
All 4 in 1

A Wild Horse Pass Novel
They Call Her Mrs. Sheriff, book 1 (A Western Romance)

Finding Love in Disaster
The Rancher's Dilemma
The Teacher's Rescue
The Soldier's Redemption

Woman of courage Series

A Love For Delicious
Ruth's Redemption
Charity's Gold Rush
Mountain Redemption
Woman of Courage series (all four books)

Short Story Westerns
Desert Rose
Desert Lilly
Desert Belle
Desert Daisy
Flowers of the Desert 4 in 1

Contemporary

Romance in Paradise
Maui Magic
Sunset Kisses
Deep Sea Love
3 in 1

Finding a Way Home
Service of Love
Hillbilly Cinderella
Unraveling Love
I'd Rather Kiss My Horse

Christmas
Dear Jillian
Romancing the Fabulous Cooper Brothers
Handcarved Christmas
The Payback Bride
Curtain Calls and Christmas Wishes
Christmas Gold
A Christmas Stamp
Snowflake Kisses
Merry's Secret Santa
A Christmas Deception

The Red Hat's Club (Contemporary novellas)

Finally
Suddenly
Surprisingly
The Red Hat's Club 3 – in 1

Short Story

One Hour (A short story thriller)
Whisper Sweet Nothings (a Valentine short romance)